Copyright © 2023 by Michael King Jr.

All Rights Reserved. No parts of this book shall be duplicated, distributed, reproduced, or photocopied without permission from the author.

This is a work of fiction. All characters, events, incidents, and places are from the author's imagination. The characters are not based upon actual persons, living or dead. The resemblance of actual persons, living or dead, is coincidental.

Acknowledgments

First off, I want to thank my mom, Anita Benton, and my dad for birthing me. I know It wasn't easy raising me, I was hard-headed and rebellious against life, but y'all never gave up on me. At times I didn't believe in myself, but y'all did. I thank y'all as well for showing me how to survive in life. We've had disagreements on certain things, but tough love is the best love when raising a man.

A special thanks go out to Alice Sims, Sharron Harris, & Danniesha Murphy! Y'all always showed me love and never turned y'all back on me. Y'all gave me a sense of hope and taught me that I always had somebody behind me, even when I felt alone. I know I was a handful, but y'all never gave up. Lastly, shout out to my Aunt Kathy. You always held a nigga down. I love y'all!

CHAPTER 1

Today was like no other day. Levelle woke up to his Uncle Icy and Uncle Tim in the kitchen, chopping it up about the next move that they were going to make. Levelle walked in on both of them loading up their handguns while discussing tonight's work. Soon as they saw Levelle come into the kitchen, they both greeted him and gave him $200 a piece for some shoes and an outfit. It might not seem like shit, but for a 16-year-old, it was a nice amount of cash. Before Levelle left the kitchen, Icy told him, "make sure you spend that money wisely." Levelle rushes out of the kitchen. As the coast clears, Icy and Tim start back chopping it up about the lick they had planned to hit on a nigga name "Biggs." He's supposed to have plenty bricks of coke and $50,000 in cash. Now the lick will be set up by a chick name "Porsha" she was a sexy stripper that weight about 170, stood about 5"3, worked at Club Silks, and every baller in the city wanted her. Luckily she belongs to Icy! I mean, she was his bottom bitch at all cost. They have been together ever since school. It all started in the 6th grade. She has been his rock, solid since day one. Icy and Tim have been planning this lick for like three weeks. It started one night they were in the strip club. "Laying" on niggas (meaning looking for a lick). Biggs and his homies came in the club, making it rain, throwing money everywhere, and every stripper from the club ran to their VIP section, shaking their ass and moving their hips to them niggas every command. Now it was Porsha's time to dance, and of course, all eyes were on her. She was seductively moving her body! Biggs couldn't help but step onto the stage and throw money everywhere. The whole time she looked Biggs in his eyes and moved her body to the music. Soon as the song was over, Porsha picked up her money and headed toward the back of the club. When Porsha walked to the locker room to freshen up, she heard her homegirl Peaches crazy ass come in talking loud like always, hollering about how much money the nigga Biggs and his crew were throwing! Now don't get it wrong, Peaches was a bad bitch! High yellow with a fat ass, but like always, she only had one flaw... she was thirsty for money and didn't know how to keep her pussy in her pants. Porsha looked at Peaches and told her, " if they throwing that much money, why are you back here talking to me!" Peaches yelled, " because bitch, for some reason, he can't stop talking about you, so hurry up, freshen up and bring your ass out here!" Porsha freshened up and made her way out to the dance floor, but before she made it to the VIP room, she was spotted by Icy and Tim. She walked over to Icy, gave him a hug and kiss, giving him a fake lap dance to fill him in on the nigga Biggs that needed her attention so much. Icy leaned in, kissed her, and told her to hit him later. Porsha walked into the VIP room to find Biggs in there, texting on his phone while his crew was making it rain. Biggs spotted Porsha and told her to come to sit next to him. She did as she was told! Biggs was not your typical nigga! He was yellow with waves that were spinning in a 360. He weighed about 180, stood about 6"1, and was cocky as hell! He wore a Balmain outfit with shoes to match. He also had a top and bottom grill in his mouth that was made up of flawless diamonds! To top that off, this nigga wore a 41 Rolex watch with diamonds around the band of it. You can tell he was getting lots of money. She looked at him and asked him why was her services needed when there were so many other girls working the floor. His reply was first off, you sexy as hell, and I can tell either you have a balling ass nigga or you already got bank. These other hoes are too thirsty, that's a turn-off to a nigga like me! Everybody else ran here, why did you pretend a nigga wasn't even here? Porsha looked at him and smiled at him, her exact words were, "I dance by choice, and just because I strip doesn't mean I sell pussy, that's the difference they sell pussy! I strip but for not much longer. I'm in my last year of law school to become a lawyer. Biggs was shocked as fuck! Surprised, from looking at her he would have never thought she was in the law field. To be honest, he needed her around just in case he was ever busted for selling drugs. For the next couple of hours,

Porsha and Biggs stayed around talking more, to get to know each other life. Biggs broke the silence asking Porsha can he take her out. Her reply was, "I don't have any problem with that but what about your girl?" I don't do drama, I'm too grown for that! Biggs replied, "I don't have a girl," while flashing his diamonds in her face. They eventually exchanged numbers. Porsha got up to leave but before leaving Biggs gave her $500 and told her he would be waiting on her call. She walked off smiling & throwing her hips from side to side. Biggs couldn't do anything but watch her ass and the way she walked. Biggs's main man's name was "Dollar", he was a nigga getting money as well but got paid for laying niggas down. Dollar walked up to Biggs and told him after the club close and we were about to go party. We taking these hoes to the clubhouse, Biggs replied, "was, I'm about to gone head home. Tomorrow is a big day for me. Truth be told, the nigga didn't want the other stripper going back telling Porsha that he got with them and ruining shit for him & Porsha. Biggs and Dollar slapped hands and Biggs walked out of the club heading home, in deep thought about life.

CHAPTER 2

The next day, Biggs was at the house cooking up some work and getting ready for his day like always. He had already cooked up 2 keys of coke, now he was waiting on them to dry. His phone started ringing, he looked at the screen to see his right-hand man Dollar. He picked up the phone and said, "what up playboy" and started laughing. Dollar got straight to the point telling him he partied with them freaks from the club and how they kicked shit all night. Biggs was all ears until he heard the phone beep and whose name it was flashing across the screen. He clicked over so fast, Dollar didn't even realize it! Biggs trying to sound all sexy and shit, "hello sweetheart". Porsha replied "nothing just in the house relaxing at the moment, how about yourself?" His reply was, "nothing same ole getting money about to get dressed, but enough about me what are your plans for today?" Her reply was "I have nothing planned. When I get dressed I will come over. Send your address. I told you I would call you so I'm a woman of my word." Biggs replied, "I see now you going to make a nigga fall for you. I admire loyalty I'm about to text you my address so you can come over. Porsha replied with a soft seductive tone "I will be over in the next hour or two", and they both ended the calls.Soon as Porsha hung up the phone she called Icy to fill him in on what was going on with her and the nigga Biggs and how he had been running his mouth about how he owned the city and don't anything or nobody move without him. Icy told her to play her part and get all the info she can get. Porsha said, "Ok baby I'm on it but you better call me later because I need to see you!" His reply was I will be over later and ended the call. Porsha hung up the phone and headed straight to her bathroom and ran a hot bubble bath so she could relax. She was still tired from working last night because she's the hottest and baddest stripper in the city and all the ballers come out to see her. When she was done running her bath she walked to her walk-in closet to see what she would be wearing for today. It was fall so she took out her Gucci sweatsuit and her Gucci shoes to match. Porsha proceeded to walk back into the bathroom after she laid her fit out. She looked in the mirror to tie knotless braids up so the water wouldn't wet them up. While sitting in the hot, relaxing bubble bath all she could think about was the last lick she set up for Icy and how it almost cost her life. Porsha was fucking with this drug dealer from Fort Smith, Arkansas. He use to come to the club when he was in town on weekends and every time he came, he hooked up with her in Pine Bluff, Arkansas. One weekend he asked her to come back home with him for the weekend and she took him up on his offer. She went out of the city with him. When they made it to his house she could tell he was getting money. His house looked like something off a movie. It was all brick, two stories, had a wrap-around driveway, and a built-in pool in the backyard. This nigga even had his own security. Well, a couple of his homies. They idolized him like this nigga was a God. He was a cool cat, but the only reason Porsha went was to please her man Icy, and set the lick up. The nigga name was Bud. He was a caramel color with long hair. He stood about 5"9 and weighed about 200 solid. He looked like he worked out. He was everything a woman wanted, but her heart was still with Icy. Porsha was laying in bed watching tv when she overheard Bud telling someone he had 200 pounds of OG Kush that had just arrived and that he would be selling the pounds for cheap. Porsha waited until the coast was clear and proceeded to shut the room door. She pulled her phone out, called Icy, and told him about the conversation she just overheard Bud talking about. She even told him about the fake bodyguards the nigga has. Icy cut her off and told her don't worry about his crew just make sure them pounds there. He also told her to tell him you want to go shopping and out to eat. He informed her they were on the way down there and ended the call. Porsha knew Icy and Tim both were straight killers. She was nervous because didn't need anyone getting hurt. At least not Icy and Tim. Porsha went downstairs and ask Bud can he take her out to eat and go shopping. His reply was, "ok baby! I'm about to take you to the best restaurant and strip mall around Fort Smith!" He told her to hold on while he went to talk to his bodyguards. Bud talked with his homies telling them to hold shit down and make sure nobody goes into the basement where the OG Kush was stored. Porsha was in the bathroom putting lip gloss on when she heard Bud calling her name and telling her he was ready to leave. Once downstairs the door was held for her and an all-white Aston Martin with 24-inch outset Forg rims sitting on it. On the way to the restaurant, they smoked, talked, and got to know each other more. Once they pulled in she noticed they were at a restaurant called 21 West End. Porsha's eyes got big because she has never been there before and it was screaming baller status. After eating a nice dinner Bud took her to the mall and let her wild out. He touched her chin and told her she could hit whatever store with an unlimited budget. On the ride home, Bud asked Porsha if she could move with him and stop stripping. Porsha's reply was, "just let things play out. I been hurt in my past and I just need time to heel. You feel me?" His reply was, "I respect that!" Before another word was exchanged they were pulling up to his luxurious home. While pulling to the front door Bud noticed it was wide open. That's something he doesn't play! His gut told him something was wrong. He pulled out his 45 pistol ready for action. Porsha's heart was racing 100 mph none stop. Bud walked into the house to find two of his homies tied up with bullet holes in the middle of their heads. He ran straight down to the basement to find all the pounds of his OG Kush were gone. He immediately went into a fucking rage. He knew it was an inside job because everyone in their right mind know not to play with Bud. He had killed plenty niggas and his dad was a mob boss back in the day. Bud ran outside, snatched the car door open, and slapped the shit out of Porsha with the butt of his gun. Blood flew everywhere! He even dragged her into the house and took her phone. At this point, Porshia was begging and screaming for her dear life, but he wasn't trying to hear that shit. He noticed one name that stood out "My Bae Icy". Once he opened the message he noticed the slick bitch took a screenshot of her location and sent it to him. He started to kill the bitch but he knew that wouldn't get his shit back. So he decided to beat her ass all night into her whole body was numb. At this point, Porsha was wishing she was dead. The next day Icy kept calling Porsha's phone back to back none stop until he got an answer, but to his surprise, it wasn't the person he wanted to hear from. The nigga Bud answered the phone. His exact words to Icy were "nigga I already know you came into my house, shit, and killed my bodyguards! You must don't know who the fuck I am?! You have 24 hours to return my shit or this bitch is dead!" and ended the call. Icy slammed the phone down so hard biting on his bottom lip with tears in his eyes. He knew his actions has caused his bottom bitch her life. Tim told Icy to calm down he has a plan that will work.

He grabbed his phone out of his pocket and called the one and only person that he knew would ride with him…Vasha. The phone rang twice and Vasha picked up saying, "hey bae". Vasha stood about 5 feet, 150 pounds, dark complexion, light green eyes, with a fat ass and flat stomach. Tim's reply was dry so she knew something was wrong. He explained what went down with Porsha and she promised him she would take care of it. Now Vasha worked for the Pine Bluff Detective Division but had connections all over. She assured Tim and Icy that she would call her homegirls in the other department and get a search warrant on the house. She told them she would call them later and they ended the call. Vasha got off the phone and her mind was racing a million places. Porsha was her homegirl back in school. They have been messing with Tim and Icy asses since grade school. She hated the fact that Porsha was a stripper but it didn't matter. All she cared about was helping Tim out he was her first love. Vasha did an NCIC (National Crime Information Center) nationwide police check and was able to pull up Bud's address. She called Tim and gave him the update. Vasha immediately told him she was on her way now! Before she could hang up the phone he told her he would have $20,000 waiting on her. Vasha replied with much emphasis in her voice, "I need more than 20k you haven't dick me down in a week!" They both started laughing and ended the call. Tim ran the playback to Icy so they can be on the same page with what was going on with Porsha but it wasn't helping

Icy keep calm any. He kept calling Porsha's phone back to back. The last few times he only got the voicemail. Later that night Bud was still at home slapping Porsha around until he saw police light surrounding his whole house and heard his door being kicked in. His initial thought was to kill Porsha but the police rushed in too fast. Vasha was the first one to approach with her 40 Glock drown ready to shoot. She gave him a fair warning to drop the gun or she will shoot. Bud looked at the odds and lowered his weapon. The other police ran and cuffed him. That was the happiest day of Porsha's life you should have seen her. She had blood running down her face and both of her eyes both were swollen shut. Her forehead was busted and she had rip-like cuts running down her body. Her clothing was ripped off and she can barely move. Vasha called the ambulance to get Porsha's help before she died because she had lost so much blood. Once getting Porsha loaded into the ambulance Vasha headed toward Fort Smith Police Department to book Bud in on charges of kidnapping, attempted murder, rape, and two more charges of murder for the two bodyguards that were killed in the house.

From that day forward she made a promise to never set up another lick for nobody, but all that was replaced with greed because the $50,000 profit she had gotten from Icy had her living good to this day.

CHAPTER 3

Porsha was bought out of deep thought to her phone ringing. She looked at the screen to find Peaches name flashing across the screen. She picked it up smiling because she knew her girl was about to pop her shit. Peaches were running her mouth none stop talking about how she, Dollar, and a couple more strippers had fun and how them niggas tricked off good. Porsha's reply was, "I hope you hoes wore a condom! Y'all don't know them niggas! Y'all hoes just met them niggas last night!" Peaches reply was, "you know I made him strap up! Anyways what are you about to do?" Changing the subject... Porsha replied, " nothing girl the nigga Biggs want me to come chill with him so that's my plan. You know I break these nigga reciting "City Girls" song real life bitch give a fuck bout a nigga period! " They both started laughing. Peaches told her she would see her at work later and they ended the call. When Porsha got off the phone she got dressed, did her makeup, and headed out the door. She got in her all-white 2019 Honda Accord and drove to Biggs house lip singing BIG OLE FREAK by Megan the Stallion. Upon arriving at his house she noticed a 2018 Range Rover truck sitting on a set of off-set forg rims, a Bentley, and a newer model Tahoe with a dark tint. Her first thought was dope boys kept shit like that to blend in traffic with the police. The house was all brick and had a 4-car garage and a wrap-around driveway. Anybody can tell this nigga was balling, but nothing like her old nigga Bud. She took her phone out text Biggs and told him she was outside. Before she could open her door Biggs was stepping outside with a white blue and red polo jumpsuit on. She couldn't stop looking him up and down. He was sexy as hell to her. She proceeded to exit her car and walked into the house right behind Biggs who lead her into his living room. Biggs had his house flushed out! He had all-white leather couches that wrapped around the whole wall, he also had a 75-inch curve tv, a black and white mink rug that sat in the middle of the floor, and decorative pictures that hung neatly on the wall. Biggs even gave her a view of the kitchen. It was also neatly organized with a marble top island kitchen and stainless steel everything to match. After Biggs gave Porsha the tour of the house he went back to the living room sat next to her and welcomed her to his castle. Porsha was very impressed but didn't want to seem like a groupie so she replied with, "I bet all your little hoes like all this!" and gave him a smirk. Biggs looked her up and down and told her "with all due respect if I viewed you as a hoe we would be at a hotel, not my house believe it or not I see something special in you and I hope my gut not leading me wrong. Every king needs a queen. I'm sure you can relate to that the last thing!" She wasn't expecting him to say those words and from that moment on she viewed him differently. She had to respect him because with his money and looks alone he could have any woman walking but what she couldn't understand was why is he single. Before she could say a word Biggs told her to follow him to the hallway so he could show her something. When he stepped in front of the picture she could tell something terrible had happened because his face soften up and his hand began to tremble. She grabbed him by the waist and asked him if he was ok? His reply was, "I'm ok", and he explained to her about the day his family was coming to see him in prison and was hit by an 18-wheeler. The truck blew up and they were pronounced dead at the scene. At that moment Biggs began to break down and cry telling her how everything was his fault and how if he wasn't in prison none of it wouldn't have happened. Porsha was devastated and hurt and all she could do is kiss his lips and tell him everything will be ok. Truth be told she couldn't relate to his situation. Biggs asked her to come sit back down so he could ease his mind and snap back to reality. He pulled out the exotic weed, rolled it up, and fired it up. After taking a couple of pulls off the weed Porsha broke the silence. She told him about her childhood and how she wanted to escape poverty by becoming a lawyer. She also told him how she was tired of working at the strip club, but that was the only thing that paid her bills. Biggs turned to face Porsha looking her dead in her eyes and said," If you show me your loyalty it won't be anything in this world that you will want for! I can take care of all your money problems. Plus I need a good lawyer and lover on my team!" She hit him playfully on the arm and gave him a smirk. Her laughter was cut short by Biggs phone ringing. When he looked at the screen it was his homie, Larry. He answered the phone saying, " What it do my boy?" Larry's reply was, "what it do bro? I need another two bricks before I run out. Money good!" Biggs's reply was, "say less I will be over in 20 mins" and ended the call. After ending the call Biggs walked into the kitchen to check to see if the dope was finished drying. He grabbed his triple beam scale to see if the dope had lost or gained. Most of the time he cooked the work himself unless somebody requested it soft therefore no one could call back complaining. He weighed the work up to find the scale reading 1,224 grams which jumped over a whole 9 pieces. He weighed the other batch to see that other weighing in at 1,218 grams which was still good. Biggs processed to put the 2 bricks in the black shopping sack and asked Porsha do she want to ride with him. Her reply was, "Sure baby I don't mind" and followed him to the door. Before leaving he set the alarm and shut the door, but what he didn't know was Porsha saw the alarm code. Big mistake... They headed out and got in his all-white Range Rover and proceeded to drive while bumping "Sada". They were vibing, smoking the exotic weed, and nodding their heads to the beat the whole way to Larry's house. When they pulled up Porsha was amazed at how the condo sat back off the lake with neatly cut grass that manicured the yard. Biggs pulled out his phone and told his homie Larry he was outside. Larry got in the backseat and got straight down to business. He gave Biggs a bag filled with $60,000 and told him he would call him in a couple of days. Biggs reply was, "ok bro you know it's love and you know that's the best shit around so get at me!" They proceed to "dap" it up and Larry got out of the truck. When Biggs drove off he asked Porsha was she hungry. Her reply was, "a little I guess a bite won't hurt". His reply was, "I have the perfect spot. You're going to love it. He lit the exotic weed back up played the system loud and headed toward the restaurant. Upon arriving at Cole's Steakhouse they noticed the line was wrapped around the corner and there were plenty of couples holding hands smiling, flirting, and just enjoying each other company. However to be so packed the line moved quickly. Porsha and Biggs were next up in line to be seated. She was all smiles because the place was amazing.The waitress was very nice and their table was set in the middle of the restaurant it was a very good view of the place. Porsha was very impressed. It had a live band playing jazz and flat screens that wrapped the whole restaurant.Posha leaned over and asked Biggs was this his first time coming there? and how did you hear about this place. His reply was this was my wife favorite spot and this is where I found my plug he say he used to come here to relax and listen to jazz bands The waitress walked up and asked them how may she help them. Biggs was the first to reply. He told the waitress to give them two blue mutherfucker drinks. While waiting on their drinks old couples walked by smiling telling them how cute they were together Porsha was all smiles.The waitress came back with the drinks they ordered and asked them what would their food of choice be. Porsha ordered a steak, shrimp, and loaded potato platter, and Biggs ordered the same thing well done to be exact. The waitress sat the 6 butter rolls down with butter that was melted across the top she told them their food will be served in 25 minutes or before she picked their menus up and walked away.While waiting on their food they sipped and talked Porsha could feel the drinks kicking in so she leaned over to ask Biggs why do they call the drinks blue mutherfuckers and why does it taste so good? He couldn't do anything but laugh none stop. He told her this was the best drink they serve and believe it will have her feeling good once it was gone Porsha just smiled and kept getting her sip on. The food arrived right on time plus he didn't want her getting drunk on an empty stomach the waitress laid the food down and asked them was everything ok? They both replied at the same time yes the waitress placed their silverware on the table and walked away.Biggs was eating a piece of steak when he noticed she haven't said a word he broke the silence saying this food too good? Her reply was yes bae I was just about to say the same thing they both start laughing and kept eating. Biggs kept eating staring at her the whole time he couldn't help but ask the question he had been wanting to ask her which was what made you want to become a lawyer? Her reply was my brother kept getting locked up so I saw firsthand how dirty the system was. My parents use to bail him out, buy him the best lawyer money could buy until one day I and my family was at home with my brother and the police came kicking our door in and talking about he was just involved in a robbery that tore my family up because my brother had been at home all day his Lil friends just was trying to beat their charges and blamed my brother for a crime he didn't do in plus I'm from the hood I saw so many dope boys pay lawyers and still go to prison one thing I promise in law is I will always do my best to win a case. Biggs and Porsha ate the rest of the food paid the waitress and headed out of the restaurant. Once they made it to the truck he could tell she was tipsy they talked the whole ride home when they pulled back up to Biggs's house he offered to take her home but she declined his request. She even told him she even wants to keep him company for a little. While he cut the Rover off Biggs grabbed the 60,000 from the backseat that he just got made from Larry. He walked around opened her door up and lead the way into the house once inside Posha was all over him rubbing on his abs he lead the way to the living room and cut the stereo on playing Tank "when we fuck played loud throughout the house to set the mood he lowered the lights with the remote grabbed Posha and they slow danced for a few minutes he cupped her ass and started kissing her slowly on the neck Porsha let out a small moan her Pussy was was soaking wet she was so tipsy and relax she couldn't control herself he was kissing him and rubbing his dick. Biggs lead the way to his room once inside he told her to take her clothes off Jacques and Def loaf came booming through the speakers of the song" Red Light".He couldn't do anything but admire her body. Her curves were on point she looked like Lisa Ray on players club. He couldn't hold back any longer. He laid her back on the bed, and start kissing her pussy while rubbing her clit at the same time. He proceeds to lick up her body at start sucking her titties. Porsha started hollering his name and pulling his head deeper she was rotating her hips holla his name and climax he climbed on top of her and slid his dick in she was biting her bottom lip he flip her doggy style and hitting her faster and faster the slow stroking her the had sex all night until they both past out.

CHAPTER 4

The next day Porsha woke up to the smell of breakfast food cooking and slow music still playing though out the house she reached over to the nightstand got her phone and noticed she had 20 missed calls all from Peaches, Icy, and her boss Ron she also had like 10 texts she had such a nice time she got drunk made love and overslept for work. While checking her text messages Biggs walks into the room with her breakfast neatly prepared he had pancakes, sausage, oatmeal, and orange juice she couldn't lie the food tasted so good he even gave her a bc to smooth the hangover that they had from the night before.He sat next to PoshaPorsha rubber the hair off her forehead and told her how he enjoyed her company and how he respected her hustle so it was her choice to get dancing he had her back either way not that I'm trying to rush you in a relationship I just love our vibe give it time think and get back to me.Porsha was speechless she didn't know what to say nor do yeah she loved Icy with all her heart and had been with him a lot of years but he never made her feel this special here it was she was sent to set this nigga up for the love of her life and here it was she was catching feelings for this nigga. When Porsha was done eating he grabbed her plate placed a rolled-up blunt on the bed and told her she had brand-new panties sitting next to the shower he even had women's body wash. He's a keeper. While heading to the shower she noticed her phone rang it was Peaches calling so she asked with a soft tone but Peaches were all over her ass saying bitch that dick must be good?I been calling you all night Ron said he called and Icy blew my shit up Porsha reply was for your info yes the dick was good this nigga ate my pussy like a snack in plus he know how to treat a real queen he took me out last night we came back to the house he dickeddicked me down and even cooked me breakfast this morning Peaches cut her saying now you know the rules don't let no nigga throw you off your game all niggas start off playing their role good then jump on some bull shit when they think they got you but hit I got to go I need some rest I love you and I will see you at work tonight and they ended the call Porsha got off the phone got in the shower thinking about what Peaches was saying she was right every nigga start off cool then jump on some bull shit in plus she didn't have time for a nigga between work ,and school but she could use a little side money and some bomb ass sex whenever Icy was playing games which was always and she was getting tired of it here it was she was there to set up a lick and was falling in love she told herself you got to be more careful. Porsha got out of the shower put her clothes on and walked into the kitchen where Biggs was standing cooking keys of coke he was so busy stirring the coke up that he didn't even notice her walking in until she wrapped her arm around his waist he turned kissed her and kept cooking the coke.Porsha told him how much she enjoyed last night and how she was looking forward to seeing him again. His reply was I hope to see you soon as well he turned around and started kissing her and squeezing her ass. They were caught in the moment until she told him she got to get ready for class. She told him she will call him later. Before she could leave he reached into the Gucci bag that held the $60,000 in it and gave her $1,000 and some of the exotic weed that he had been smoking. He told her to go shopping and to get whatever she need. She was so happy she gave him a hug and another kiss, put the weed in her purse, and walked out the door. When Porsha got in the car she fired one up and drove off she called Icy phone 2 times he picked up saying you must had a blast last night? Her reply was it wasn't anything like that I fell asleep at the nigga house we went and had drinks I road with him to pick up money and drop off work but I don't know how must it was I just know he dropped off two big blocks of work off to some nigga name Larry ho stay in some condos by the lake you know I got you so don't do that there's nothing to worry about Icy I will never love another man on earth the way I love you I'm about to head home and get ready for class when I get out I will call you if you not too busy? Icy replied with ok with a slick attitude and hung up the phone she know he was mad but she didn't care she was trying to help him out.Icy had the phone on speakerphone the whole time talking to Porsha he needed Tim to be the judge of things instead of him so he looked at Tim and asked him what did he think?Tim gave him his honest opinion I think she is falling for the nigga Biggs so you going to have to snap her back to reality he probably took her out showed her a good time dicked her down word around town that nigga got plenty of Money a bro we can't mess up this lick behind Porsha trying to catch feelings for a nigga.Icy know Tim was right so he made a note to himself to check Porsha later before things got out of hand.Porsha pulled up to her apt feeling good she can't believe she pulled a real boss that's willing to take care of her on one hand she was tired of working at the strip club but on the other hand it paid her bills so she couldn't complain she had all type of thoughts running threw her Mind she also thought about Icy and how her love ran deep for him she ran bath water to soak she listen to slow music got dressed and headed out for class.

CHAPTER 5

Levelle came home from school him his right-hand man Carlos they grew up together in the same hood as they made it in the house Icy and Tim were just leaving home like always Levelle told Carlos to follow him to the basement so he could show him his uncle guns they had just bought some Ar pistols handguns, Glock 40's, and some bulletproof vest as well. Levelle held the 40 Glock and handed the Ar to Carlos now if anybody fuck with us we got these to fuck them up on my dead momma now let's put these back up before Unk them come back tripping. They went straight to playing NBA live on the PlayStation. Something they did after school every day. Levelle loved the Lakers while Carlos loved the Bucks. They were playing the game intensely until they heard gunshots ring through the windows. They both ducked down until the shooting stopped. Levelle lead the way downstairs to the basement where they both grabbed the guns and ran outside. When they made it the shooters were already gone. Icy and Tim were pulling up in their yard when they noticed Levelle and Carlos were outside with guns drown out in plain site Levelle spoke with anger in his voice his exact words were somebody just came through this bitch shooting you see the holes in the window? You could hear sirens approaching so Icy grabbed the guns told everyone to get in the car and drove off at a high rate of speed they already had a clue of who it could be because they had just robbed a nigga name Trae Trae after the club last weekend he was fronting well with about $20,000 in all hundreds on him, drunk talking all loud like he was untouchable. The nigga was always on some loud-talking shit, but little did he know tonight was the night. Icy looks at Tim and tells him man we should have just killed the nigga. Tim's reply was, "you right bro. That nigga probably paid somebody to come shoot our shit up since we killed his two right-hand mans the other night. Plus that nigga ain't got the balls to come play with us!" Icy reply was, "we should have known this shit would happen. What nigga gets robbed for $20,000, main man gets killed and he doesn't retaliate? Never forget a pussy nigga will kill you! Next nigga we stick up we going to kill!" Tim told Icy to watch what he said in front of Levelle and Tim the last thing they needed was them little niggas running their mouths. Icy was so mad he told Levelle next time you go snooping around in our shit and some shit like this happens and you don't use it I'm going to beat your ass do you understand me? Levelle's reply was, "my bad Unk they were gone when we made it outside. They pulled up at Carlos's house and told Levelle they would be back to get him later before leaving." Tim gave him a couple of dollars. After pulling off Tim told Icy to never talk to Levelle like that we were supposed to be looking out for him. He has already been through a lot and the last thing we need is for his dropping out of school, robbing, and selling dope like us.Levelle's mother's name was Tiffany she was the oldest sister of the 3 until she passed away from cancer she was like a mother to the brothers. She cooked, cleaned, and came and came and saw both of them when they were in prison a while back for robbing the hood corner store. Icy pulls up in the yard to find police cars everywhere like it was a murder scene. When they made it out of the car they were approached by Tim's girlfriend Tavasha Sims and detective Chris Shelton. He stood about 6 feet and weighed about 220 pounds. Tim never liked Chris because mainly he thought he was too tuff, but really Chris played Tuff behind the police badge. What he didn't know was Tim could get him touched at any moment. All he had to do was press the issue to Vasha ass hard enough. Detectives Chris Shelton was the first one to speak like always his exact word were what the fuck y'all got going on around here? Tim's reply was, "nigga can't you see we just pulled up. If we were here there would be dead bodies laying all over this bitch." Chris's reply was, "every time I look around y'all got some bullshit jumping off! Now tell me who the fuck have y'all been into it with lately?" Tim's reply was, "like I told you before we don't know who, and besides, do I look like a rat to you? Besides I don't let the police handle my business!" He walked a little closer to Chris but Icy and Tim stepped between them before things got out of hand out there. Before Chris could walk off he put a grin on his face looked both of them up and down and said they should have killed y'all gang-banging ass Tim's reply was why don't you do it with your tuff ass. Chris just walked away like he didn't even hear him. When Chris was out of eyesight Vasha told them to chill out. I know y'all going to handle y'all business but do it smart and Tim why you always got to get into with Chris? You know his ass but he still works for the police and never alert the Opps. And to y'all he the oops! Vasha walked off to find more out about the investigation. When Vasha walked away Icy looked at Tim and told him he talk too much. Here it is you got a down bitch on the police force who will do anything for you but you keep putting her in fucked up positions to choose between you and her job. I think you are worried she fucking that nigga Chris. What you don't know won't hurt you bro. Tim looked at Icy and told him you right bro but you know I hate police and he always acting Tuff now let's get out of here before he looks in the car and try to lock us up.

CHAPTER 6

Biggs was at the house chilling smoking talking shit with his right-hand man Dollar they were counting the money up in the money machine so everything would be intact for when their plug Rico called. After counting up all the money it was like $800,000. Biggs still had 4 bricks left over and at least 16 zips of work that was already cooked. He gave Dollar 2 bricks of coke. Dollar has to eat at all cost… He had to make sure he ate just like himself. Biggs told Dollar he might want to take it slow with the work because Rico ass hasn't called back yet and ain't no telling when he will. Dollar's reply was big bro ain't no taking it slow. Once this shit gone I'm cashing out like always. Aye but let me holler at you about something real quick man to man on some real shit. I see you feeling the chick Porsha. I ain't gone lie shorty fine, but don't move too fast. You my guy and I love you to death and I will hate to kill a stripper behind you. I'm not saying she like that but you can't be too sure. Anyway, I'm going to do a background check on her to see what's up with her. I just wanted to get that off my chest. Biggs soaks up every word Dollar was saying and had a good point.

When a nigga feels lonely he will do anything for love and will move a little too fast. But it was something about Porsha he liked. Biggs hit the blunt passed it to Dollar and told him on some real shit thank you I will take your advice and you know I love you too like my own brother but I ain't gone lie shorty bad and that Pussy fire as hell they both broke up out into laughter. Biggs looked at his watch and told Dollar to let's go get something to eat I'm starving and haven't eaten since this morning.Before leaving Biggs set the alarm like always they jumped in the drop Bentley he dropped the top since it was feeling nice outside to be fall. Once I the way to the restaurant they played "East Side Pezzy no hook". Biggs's cell phone rings it was Porsha calling he picked up so fast Dollar could tell it was Porsha because his guy was smiling from ear to ear. Biggs was on the phone asking Porsha what was she doing. Her reply was, nothing just got out of class. What about you baby? His reply was me and Dollar about to go out to eat. Call your homegirl and see if she wants to come out to eat. We're going to Chili's by Walmart. Her reply was okay let me call her and we will be up there in a little while, and ended the call. Biggs hung up the phone and told Dollar that was Porsha and she said she was about to go get Peaches ass and pull up on us. After that we taking them back to the house. We ain't got shit to do until Rico calls back anyways whenever he makes it back to town. Lil bro I can't wait until we get rich so we can take trips and enjoy life. This shit ain't called living. Them niggas stay all over the country. Dollar starts laughing loudly. His exact words were, "Biggs you got over 5 million put up plus this hustle... you good!" Biggs's reply was, "bro the more money you get the more you want. This shit didn't happen overnight and you know the loss I took to get this shit." Porsha called Peaches phone while she drove off from her school. Her phone rang two times. She answered like she was in the shower or something. Porsha was like girl what are you doing getting fucked in the shower? Porsha's reply was putting some clothes on. I'm about to come pick you up. Biggs and Dollar ass want us to come out with them and girl let me tell you he gave me $1,000 to go shopping before I left him earlier. This nigga really trying to cuff me up but hurry up I will be there in 10 mins I have to stop at the store to get some backwoods to roll up. Peaches reply was I'm getting out of the shower now and they ended the call. Porsha pulled in front of Peaches house listening to Carli B. She really was feeling herself. She parked the car, got out, walked up to the house, and knocked on the door. Peaches opened the door wearing a channel jumpsuit with the channel fluffy channel flip flops on. She even had her body wave bundles in. Porsha couldn't lie, her friend was fine. Peaches told her to walk into the house grabbed her weed and they both headed toward the car. On the way to chili's Porsha fired up the exotic weed that she got from Biggs Peaches was running her mouth about how much fun with Dollar the other night but she know he wasn't trying to fuck with her on that level she also told Porsha she wasn't t trying to settle down any time soon in plus the strip club was here man at least it paid her bills. Porsha's reply was, "I love dancing too but I can't keep dancing the rest of my life hell I got one more year before I become I lawyer. I know that's going to be my way out of this game. A but for real this nigga Biggs is cool and all but I'm just dealing with him until I can set him up for Icy ass." You should have seen the look on Peaches face. Her exact words were, so you fucking this nigga just to set up a lick for Icy broke ass? You must forgot what happened last time! You almost lost your fucking life! Fuck that broke-ass nigga girl! You have to start thinking about yourself more. All Porsha could do is let the shit she was saying go in one ear and out the other. By the time they spoke again they were pulling up to Chili's. Soon as they arrived Porsha parked, pulled out her phone, and texted Biggs telling him and Dollar that her and her girl were outside. Biggs replied back fast, we are standing at the front door. You will see us. Just come on. At first, she didn't know what car he was driving until she spotted his Bentley sitting pretty with the forg rims sitting on it. She pointed at his car and told Peaches girl this is how he riding. His car is so pretty ain't it? Peaches reply was girl it's real nice. I ain't know he was doing it like that. He must be pushing keys of dope to be riding like that. Porsha's reply was girl I told you I can't wait until you see his house now come on before they think we got lost and plus

I'm starving. Once inside the restaurant, they sat down. Dollar and Peaches were smiling from ear to ear the whole vibe was right. Biggs broke the silence telling the ladies they look nice tonight. I thought some models were walking through the door. Everyone starts laughing. Porsha hit his arm playfully and told him bae stop playing so much but thanks. The waitress walked up and ask were they ready to order. But for some reason, you could tell she had a little attitude. She kept looking Biggs all in his face but didn't say a word. She took everyone's order and walked away. When the waitress walked away Peaches was the first to speak saying what's wrong with that waitress bitch? She showl looking lost. Porsha's reply was girl don't start! We come to have fun! Before any more words could be exchanged the waitress returned with their four drinks of Long Island ice tea. She asked were they ready to order. Biggs's reply was come back in ten minutes and we would be ready to order. The waitress replied okay and walked away smiling.

CHAPTER 7

Levelle and Carlos were back at the house playing the game and talking about the shooting that occurred earlier Levelle looked over at Carlos and told him I wish we would have killed them bitch ass niggas. I don't know who the fuck they think we are! That's why we need to get our guns ASAP because Unk them ain't going to always be there and we need to stand our own ground and then Unk them won't talk to take to us like we some pussies. I have been wanting to take my anger out on somebody ever since my mom died. That took all the love from me. We also need to come up with our own hustle my mom is dead, your mom is on dope, and both our pops be in and out of prison. I'm tired of asking Unk them for money. We need our money fuck handouts. Carlos's reply was we need to find some dope to sell do you still have the money saved up from Icy and Tim? His reply was yes. Carlos told him okay we need to buy some guns and kill them niggas before Unk them make it to them. That will show them we ain't no pussies. We need to start robbing niggas! Why sell dope when we can get the whole bag? Levelle couldn't do anything but smile his main man was right it was time to step up the only problems he will have is his uncles but they will grow to love him more once he show his loyalty. Carlos's mom came into the room like always asking do they have any money. Levelle reaches into his pocket like always and gave her 20 dollars. You could tell it pissed Carlos off but he downplayed it. One thing about Levelle he was big on taking care of your mom since he no longer had one.

CHAPTER 8

Vasha walked out of Tim and icy sister's house with a yellow envelope full of evidence it was busted glass, bullet shells casings, and a couple of guns Chris wanted to take them to jail but Vasha reminded him that they didn't have a search warrant she was the lead detective in charge and he hated that he had to follow her lead she was cursing Tim out in her head she always told him about leaving guns laying out all she could do is think about Levelle luckily he wasn't there when they arrived or they would have to turn it over to the department of human services he was already going through so much with his mother being dead.Vasha knew Tim and Icy would handle their business and one thing she knew was they would never snitch one thing she hated was rats ever since her dad got a life sentence from his best friend telling on him after a robbery back in the days that was the last time she saw her dad free. Vasha had so many dope boys calling her phone on the low trying to work out deals or set people up that's what she respected the most about Icy and Tim they were stump-down killers even when they got caught for the store robbing neither one of them ratted they took their time went did their Tim and was back home in no time. On the way back to the detective station she calls Tim to tell him about the guns that were found in the house she also told him that she knew he was going to retaliate but she needs him to be smart about it his reply was I'm cool baby but do you think we can get them guns back? Her reply was boy I will see what I can do at least your ass free fuck these guns if Chris wasn't here I can do something but you know I don't trust his ass baby I will call you later so answer the phone?His reply was I love you and dome a favor get Lil Trae Trae's address from the north that's who shot the house up we got into it at the club and ended the call. Tim and Icy drove back to their ducked-off apt, well at least they think it's lowkey... to get their thoughts together. They were taking shots of Hennessy and were smoking blunts. Tim was snorting coke, something he did from time to time. One thing for sure is they didn't tolerate disrespect. An hour had gone by and Porsha still haven't called. He knew she was out of class so he shot her a text that read "I see you haven't called nor texted me back yet. any other time I couldn't keep you from blowing up my phone so you can play these little games all you want! Seem like you slick falling in love with the nigga! I will find both of y'all and kill you bitch and you know I'm not playing." Porsha phone vibrated in her purse she took it out unlocked it and read the text from Icy after reading it her stomach got weak one thing for sure is this nigga was not to be fucked with she asked Biggs to let her up from the table she told him she will be right back she had to use the restroom she was so nervous she ran in the stall pull her phone out and dialed Ivy number. The phone barely rung and he picked up saying hello in a real angry tone of voice you could tell something was wrong from how he sounded Porsha got straight to the point bae you know I ain't trying to play you and I ain't falling for no nigga but you I'm just doing what you told me to do I'm out eating with him at chili's he brung his homeboy so i bought Peaches with me but I haven't told her shit I know she talk to much Ivy cut her off yeah don't tell that bitch shit with her thristy thirsty ass I'm just a little upset right now somebody cane and shoot up our house today while Levelle and his little friend was there you know someone is going to die tonight but I will come to the club later and holler at you ? Porsha's reply was be careful bae I love you and do you need my house key? Because you know I will be hurt if something happens to Levelle how about you let him come stay at my place tonight plus he has to get up from school his reply was naw he's good I will see you later and ended the call.Porsha went back to the table and sat down but her whole vibe was off no one could tell but Peaches they have been around each other their whole life luckily the waitress had brought the ticket out Biggs looked at the ticket went in his pocket and gave her 200 dollars grabbed Porsha by the waist but for some reason, she kept noticing how the waitress was looking at him with a mug on her face either they had already fucked or the bitch was downright crazy now don't get shot twisted the waitress was fine redbone with a plump ass but you could tell she was younger she had no stomach she also had light hazel eyes really if they are fucking Biggs could have told me I might would have fucked her with him. When they made it to the front lobby Biggs wrapped his arms around Porsha he whispered in her ear telling her how he wanted to eat her pussy and how he wanted her to ride his dick before she went to work her reply was I will be over in a min is it cool for me to bring Peaches? His reply was she's cool bring her. Me and Dollar will be waiting on y'all. He kissed her on her back and told her to hurry. Porsha couldn't lie the way he kissed her had her pussy soaking wet. There was something about him that kept her horny. Biggs and Dollar got in the Bentley fired up a blunt and headed toward the house they had "Lil baby no friends "bumping through the speakers when they arrived home Dollar looks and tell Biggs damn if peaches wasn't a stripper I would fuck with her tuff. she was rocking the hell out of that dress! shorty got a banging body on her! Biggs's reply was, "yeah bro she is banging." Biggs unset the alarm and they walked into the house he asked Dollar to help him put the money on the table up because he didn't know Peaches enough to be showing her money and dope. He has already been showing Porsha too much. When they were done he cut the surround sound on and placed a bottle of Hennessy on the table he told Dollar to roll a couple of blunts because lil momma them about to come over. Biggs looked at Dollar and said, "I don't know about you but I'm about to get my fuck on!" They both started laughing and all yeah did you see how Trina was looking when we were at Chili's? Dollar's reply was hell yeah I'm surprised she didn't snap out she was mad but she kept it, player, you got to respect that .now Trina was Biggs little side chick he was fucking her until she started to become too obsessed so he had to put her on the bench for a minute. Porsha and Peaches were almost at Biggs house they were dancing and lip-singing to "City girls big ole freak "until Porsha cut the radio down looked at Peaches and asked her did she see the way the waitress was looking at Biggs. Her reply was girl something wasn't right with that but so what fuck them niggas we just want the money she can have the niggas Porsha's reply was I know right girl but let me tell you why I came back looking crazy Icy texted me talking about somebody came and shot up his house he on some bull shit then he acting all jealous and shit talking about I'm falling in love with the nigga Biggs when he the one told me to play this nigga close he sat him and Tim coming by the club later I can tell he been drinking I ain't got time for this shit tonight. Peaches look over at her and tell her straight up fuck icy if he comes in there tripping tonight I'm going to cuss his ass out I'm tired of his broke ass Porsha cut her off and said girl shut up now let's go in here and chill for a minute we got work in a few.Peaches looked at the house they stopped in front of and said damn this a big house I see why you like this nigga he bossed up! And who pretty ass Range Rover is that? Porsha's reply was girl all them cars are his now come on with your thirsty ass! They got out of the car and walked to the door it was already cracked open I guess he was watching us pull up. When they made it inside Biggs and Dollar were sitting at the table pouring shots and smoking blunts they had the speakers up loud bumping that new " Money Bagg Yo Biggs handed them shot glasses and told them to relax he gave them blunts and told them to fire up they laughed, danced and partied for the next hour Biggs was feeling drunk and horny so he asked Porsha and Peaches have they seen the new movie plug love? Their reply was we heard of it but never saw it he killed the music put the movie in and dimmed the lights. They began watching the movie until Biggs started kissing Porsha's neck he could tell she was horny so he told her to follow him to the room soon as they made it they were all over each other. Her whole body was trembling. He pulls his shirt off and pants down Porsha could barely move the feeling of him touching her was too intense he took her clothes off laid her down and started kissing her pussy she was rotating her hips. His mouth steadily moshing his name dam Biggs lick me right there kiss me dan baby he ate her for at least 39 minutes straight her legs were shaking and she was calling his name louder and louder. Porsha tells him to lay back she started sucking his dick deep throating him and spitting on it at the same time she sucked him for at least 10 minutes then she climbed on top and fucked him. she got on her tip toes and was riding him fast then slow he was slapping her in the ass and sucking on her neck. Peaches could hear the way her friend was moaning it made her wet it seem like Porsha was getting louder so Dollar asked if she could follow him to the guest room. Soon as they made it Peaches took her clothes off and started sucking his dick she was gagging and slurping at the same time boss head he felt himself about to but so he flipped her over and started hitting her fast from the back all he could think is this stripper bitch the real goat he fucked her in all type of potions for the next hours when they were done their whole body was drenched in sweat. Biggs and Porsha were laying in the bed kissing when his phone went off he looked at the screen and noticed it was a text from Trina that read " baby I'm sorry I learned my lesson now come see me I won't bug you again you know I miss you it hurt me to see you with another female text me when you can. Porsha got up and headed toward the shower to wash off the last thing she needs is to get pregnant by Biggs she haven't taken her shot in 3 months she was in the shower for about 15 minutes Biggs was steadily texting Trina until he heard the shower cut off so he put his phone down and fired up a blunt. Porsha walked Into the room looking sexy as hell he couldn't do anything but start sucking in her neck she was that fine he wanted to go another round but she drove him telling him bae you know I have to work? You going to have me late his reply was baby you know I can't help myself around you then passed her the blunt. Biggs asked her if she was coming home tonight. To herself, she couldn't believe he said home but her reply was bae yes if you still up I work late so we will see.Peaches were walking out of the bathroom when Porsha was walking out of the room she asked her if was she ready to go. Peaches reply was yes girl let me get my purse out of the room. she walked into the room and tell Dollar to call her he kissed her. Soon as they left Porsha was the first to speak girl that nigga ate the fuck out of my pussy Peaches replied girl I heard you in there y'all were loud but that nigga Dollar must popped an x pill the way he fucked me? They both were laughing and talking the whole way home. Porsha pulls up to Peaches house to drop her off before she could get out Porsha told her that she will see her at work later Peaches replies okay girl and don't be late because Ron has been on some bullshit lately.

CHAPTER 9

Icy and Tim walked out their apt jumped in the trap car dressed in all black they had got a phone call telling them Trae Trae's little cousins were the ones who cane shot up their house Tim had already gotten into with them a couple of months back over their little sister Lil Red her and Tim were fucking around tuff until he caught her trying to go in his stash and take a couple of hundreds he slapped her up and kicked her ass out she called her four brothers like they see tuff so he called Icy. Lil red was a bad yellow bone and had a petite frame weighing about 140 with sandy red hair she was sexy as hell Icy told Tim not to trust her but he kept messing with her. Icy pulled up and jumped out with his gun Lil Red brothers were Lou talking but nothing went down that day he told Tim to watch then hating ass nigga but his reply was fuck then niggas they know what's up shit seemed cool until they robbed Trae Trae bitch ass.Now somebody was calling Tim's phone talking about what they were going to do Icy told him to hang up and don't argue with anybody on the phone let's just go by Ox house he had been steadily calling saying he got them Fn's pistols for us he sake we can buy them for 700 a piece. They pulled up to Ox's house to find him sitting on the porch with Lil Ox when he saw the car he was clutching no one knew their car because it was a trap only time they drove it is to do robberies and murders Tim let down the tinted windows so Ox wouldn't shoot. Soon Ox saw their face he came to the car showing love. he told them nigga I almost started shootings I didn't know who y'all was.Icy reply was I'm glad you didn't. You know this the low and we don't drive this until it's real. Ox told his son to go inside he know something was wrong. Ox told them to come inside the house he got what they need they walked in to find Lil ox sitting in the living room playing the game both of them gave him a 20 a piece and headed into the room where Ox was. Once inside Ox told them to lock the door he pulled out Ak's fn's and all type of Glocks Icy told him all we need is the fn's big homies here go 1400 you know somebody cane shot up our house earlier we about to handle this shit Ox reply was what I ain't shot about this shit who the fuck was it? Tim's reply was Trae Trae Lil bitch ass we about to go handle it Ox's reply was be careful. I know I raised some killers but these niggas snitch so kill everyone. Tim's reply was you know that OG did their handshake and left out the house and got in the car. Icy walked back into the house smiling he know he raised some real killers every OG was proud of that. Icy was driving and Tim was riding shotgun they turned down 29th St. on the west side of town they passed by Ron Ron them. They were at Lil Red's brother's house. At a normal rate of speed trying to make sure everything that their source told them was true Tim spotted a white crown Vic sitting on the side of the house with the back window shot out like they had been doing some shooting and accidentally shit their own window out that's all they needed to confirm that their source was telling the truth. Tim asked Icy did he see the car sitting on the side of the house with the window shot out. Icy reply was he'll yeah I saw that shit them niggas must be stupid they pulled up a half block put their hoods on and got out of the car. While walking up to the house they noticed a car pull up they walked a little slower to see who was getting out of the car when they saw it wasn't anybody but two girls Icy and Tim ran up a little so they could catch the girls going in the house they put their guns on the back of their heads and told them to scream and we will blow your brains out what they didn't know was they were about to die anyways. They walked the girls into the house luckily it was open it was so much noise inside they knew they wouldn't be heard Icy pushed the girl so hard and they both got to shooting they walked over to the brothers trying to rub and shot his straight on the head they shot everyone in the head ran out the house got into their car and left the scene not caring who seen them. Once back at the apt it was about midnight so they knew the neighbors couldn't spot them the car wasn't in nobody's name so they weren't tripping about that they planned to take the cat to the chop shop tomorrow anyways. They pulled up and walked into the house happy it was time to celebrate from the demo they just put down they poured shots of Hennessy smoked a blunt and played the game after an hour went by avid they haven't gotten a call from the police Tim paused the game to ask Icy do he want to go to the strip club for a minute? Icy reply was hell yeah I need to holler at Porsha anyways plus you know Vasha going to be calling soon as she gets wind of the shooting.Icy headed to the shower to make sure he had the gun residue off him just in case somebody saw their face and found the shooting never can be so careful he stayed In the shower for the next 30 minutes rye got out got dressed putting on his all-black polo jumpsuit with his black and yellow 23 Jordan's on while Tim took a shower they talked about their dead sister and they both missed her. Tim stepped out of the shower wearing a blue and red polo jumpsuit with shoes to match they both grabbed 5,000 a piece out of the safe and headed for the door.

CHAPTER 10

Police arrived on the scene responding to a shooting in progress while investigating the outside t the house because no one answered the door the police entered and found dead bodies everywhere they had the whole block lit up with blue lights filled with police and detective trying to figure out a motive of the case they had 3 corners out there you could tell it something bad had happened but you couldn't tell it was 6 bodies found on the scene. Detective Chris and Vasha were working off on their shift but we were still called in due to the seriousness of the murder when they pulled up there were news reporters you call they were there to tell their side of the story first. When the two rookie detectives saw Vasha and Chris they filled them in on what happened and all the details on the crime scene Vasha already know Icy and Tim were all over this. The boys that were in the house laying dead were Trae Trae's first cousins. She grew up with them in the same hood. Killing them was cool, but why the girl had to die? Chris shook his head from side to side he walked over to the neighbors trying to get them to speak about what they saw soon as they saw him waking up everyone told him at once they didn't see anybody shooting they just heard shots that sounded like thunder. Chris wrote everyone's information in his notebook and told them he would get back to them if he needed any more information. The crime scene people were in the house wiping everything down trying to find much DNA as they could possibly find the news reporters were out there telling the world lies like always of what they thought happened but they also said there were no leads at this time. Chris walked over to Vasha and asked her what did she think? Her reply was I don't know but we are going to get to the bottom of it his reply was I think this is all connected? Referring to Icy and Tim's house getting shot up earlier her reply was now let's not jump the gun on this we can't just point them out then there is no witnesses to confirm anything he walked over toward the shot up crown Vic and asked Vasha what do she think happened to that? Her reply is I saw that I told the crime scene to get the prints whoever did this was cold-blooded killers with no heart I had them run the crown Vic but it hasn't been registered in anyone's name in years we have no fight right now this is the whole scene is giving us no clues. When they turned around they saw 3 women walking up toward the crime scene screaming, hollering, and crying they were followed by a couple of men Vasha knew Ron Ron and Lil Red's mom from being on the hood but she didn't know the other two woman she stopped them before they could reach the yellow tape asking them how may she help them? Mrs. Carlin told Vasha I'm just trying to see if my boys are in the house? With her eyes swollen shut from crying the other woman told Vasha I know my two girls were here because o just dropped them off about an hour ago. Vasha fought back tears she hated to be the one to deliver bad news she told them straight up I'm so sorry to do y'all lost but they didn't make it the boys nor the girls both women broke down hollering and kicking, you name it. The men that came with them tried to gain control. Chris walked over to Mrs. Carlin tryna to talk but was unsuccessful. heHe hugged her and told her he promised to find whoever was responsible for their loss. Vasha looked over at Chris and told him this is going to be a long night.

CHAPTER 11

Icy and Tom walked into the strip club like nothing ever happened the strippers were dancing to the music like always so they went sat next to the bae they asked the bartender to bring them a fifth of Hennessy since they were renting out the VIP section Icy reachable in his pocket and gave Tim an x pill to pop it was time to celebrate them niggas should have known better to go shoot at them. They gave the bartender 250 dollars for the Hennessy and the VIP room the bartender tried to flirt but they were giving her the time of day. Icy and Tim were in VIP rolling up when a couple of strippers walked in one name was Foxy and the other name was Star. they were fine as hell foxy went sat in Tim's lap while star went sat in Icy lap foxy was a sexy dark color with Chinese eyes she weighed about 160 5"6 with a flat stomach star was y'all standing 6"1 high yellow with stars tattoos running down the side of her right side they were having a good time smoking blunts, dancing until Porsha and Peaches walked in Icy already knew it was about to be some shit so he told the stripper he would holler at her later. Foxy was still dancing on Tim he was rubbing on her oust and kissing her neck. Porsha walked up to Icy kissed him and told him I see you having a good time with that bitch don't get her fucked up his reply was baby I don't want anybody in here but your sexy add so don't play I will be over later to fuck your brains out. Peaches and Foxy were dancing all over Tim. Peaches were hoping she and him didn't get into tonight. Her mouth was smart and he didn't like that. She could tell he was in a good mood because he was dancing and talking shit.Icy was kissing Porsha's neck but he noticed she had a hickey on it he kept cool whispering in her ear telling her I hope you didn't forget the plan with this nigga? Her reply was no baby I'm just playing my part I don't want to do it anymore I see it's starting in create problems for us. his reply was I'm just making sure you ain't falling in love with this nigga. Her reply was baby like I told you I ain't loved no man like I been loving you. I already have the nigga house code he didn't have any money sitting out. you know I'm going to tell you when it's time just like last time. his reply was yeah keep that hoe Peaches out of my business. I handled them niggas who shot up the house, but I'm still looking for Trae Trae bitch ass. Porsha got Icy on the arm and told him to look at Tim he was dancing all on peaches something he never did.They hated each other from their old relationship. they use to date until he found out she was selling pussy and stripping he left her and went back to Vasha. Icy passed the blunt to Tim reached in his pocket and pulled out a party pack of pills he gave everybody one and popped another one himself he grabbed the shot glasses off the table filled them up with Hennessy and did a toast to his brother for the demo they had put down earlier. The bartender walked in and asked everyone if were they ok? Tim reached in his pocket gave her 500 dollars and told her to bring him all ones she took his money and told him she would be right back. Foxy and Peaches were dancing all on each other Tim was sitting back like a boss enjoying the show he reached out grabbed peaches hand and led her to his lap he whispered in her ear can I have both of y'all tonight? Her reply was boy you know I'm down if she is and I miss your ass anyways shit ain't been the same ever since you dogged me out back in the days his reply was you the one who had a baby and was fucking all the homies in the hood ain't no real nigga accepting that shit but keys have fun tonight her reply was baby but foxy supposed to stay at my house tonight you can just leave with us if you not playing?Tom looked down at his phone and noticed he had missed 5 calls from Vasha he already suspected what she was calling about she shot him a text that read I know you see me calling you. I was just trying to make sure you ok? But call me back this is important I have something to tell I'm you. Tim walked over to Icy and talked his shoulder he leaned over and told him that he had 5 missed calls and she texted talking about she had something important to tell me. Icy reply was, go call her to make sure shit straight. The last thing we need is to be caught off guard. Tim grabbed the bottle of Hennessy off the table took a couple of sips and told peaches and foxy he would be right back. He walked out of the VIP heading to the restroom. before he could make it he was stopped by a stripper name Cherry whom he use to talk to. she hugged him and told him she missed him and didn't know he was in the club his reply was, come to VIP, I got you! Me and icy ass have been here for about an hour. Her reply was I will be over once I perform. I go on stage next so come make it rain baby. Tim gave her a stack of money and headed toward the restroom. when he made it in the restroom some old nigga was in there getting his hustle on he had condoms, backwoods, and phone chargers he gave the old school $50.00 and told him to step out he needed to have a private conversation with the old man took the money and rushed out the restroom. Tim locked the door took out his phone and calls Vasha's phone the phone rang twice. She picks it up saying hey baby how are you? His reply was nothing at the strip club having drunk me and icy. Her reply was I bet that bitch peaches thirsty ass better not be in your face? You know I still can't stand that stripping ass bitch but look I'm over her at this crime scene on 29th street somebody came over here and killed Ron Ron and his 3 brothers and killed 2 girls this shit is crazy the neighbors said they heard shots but didn't see anything bae be careful and I need you to come over when I get off but was about to say something but was cut off to Chris calling Vasha name she told Tim she would call him back with more information and ended the call. Tim left out the bathroom and headed back to the VIP when he got back everyone was smoking dancing and parting icy was throwing money on cherry peaches foxy and Porsha Tim walked up to icy and told him everything was good they parted for the next hour until the Dj called for the last call for liquor Porsha told icy them that she had to head to the back to pay her boss and put her clothes on icy told he will see her outside he told Tim to come on it time to leave before time got up foxy and Peaches told him that they were going straight home and would be waiting on him his reply was I will be right outside waiting. They walked out to the parking lot for a while taking and rolling blunts they were trying to give the ladies time to come out plus they were rolling off the x pills and didn't have anything better to do. Tim told Icy how he was about to go fuck Peaches and Foxy and how he had been wanting them two together icy hit the steering wheel laughing he said boy you a fool but I wish I could join them hoes fine but you know Porsha ain't going for that shit Tim looked at him with a serious look so you think she ain't fucking Biggs? Icy reply was man he can have her Pussy I got her heart before anything was said they saw the ladies coming out of the club being led out by the club security guards.They told the security the girls was good Peaches gave her keys to Foxy and told her to wait in the car Foxy did what she was told and kept walking Porsha walked up to the car so Icy let the window down she told icy that she was ready when he was ? and she headed toward the car but Tim stopped her calling her name a Porsha? Take care of my brother and don't drain him too much we got shit to do tomorrow everyone started laughing her reply was big boy can handle himself you need to be worried about Peaches and Foxy's freaky ass his reply was hell they need to be worried about me I'm the energize bunny peaches hit him playfully and told him to bring his ass in. Tim grabbed 3 rolled-up blunts got a bottle of Hennessy gave Icy's handshake like always and got out of the car and went got in with Peaches and foxy and drove off bumping "NBA Young Boy ronada. Icy followed Porsha home bumping "NBA lonely child he had the song on repeat he was in deep thought mainly about the innocent girls he just had to kill. On the way to Peaches house she cut the radio down and asked Tim and Foxy did they need any from the store. His reply was no I got two packs of swishers a pint of Hennessy and a box of rubbers so I'm good foxy was quiet it was making him paranoid because she kept texting none stop on her phone. Peaches drove straight home bumping her music and dancing when they arrived they walked straight into Peaches apt Tim had his gun drown the whole time just in case some funny shit was going on he didn't trust either one of them for all he knows it could be a set up when they made it inside he felt safe because of it was an ambush niggas would have jumped out blasting already. Peaches walked in and blue-toothed her phone to the radio she put it on "Lil Baby close friends" and asked if he was okay. Before she went to take a shower his reply was yes I'm good just bring me a cup of ice and the ashtray. Foxy was already in the bathroom taking a shower Peaches returner in the living room gave Icy the ashtray and a cup of ice she sat down on his lap kissed him and told him how she was really glad he came over he smiled and told her thanks, hit the blunt and laid back.Peaches and Foxy were washing up and kissing foxy told her to hurry up before Tim gets bored Peaches was so horny off the pills she kept rubbing foxy and kissing on her neck when they reached the front room Foxy sat next to Tim while peaches went got them two cups of ice when she returned Tim was feeling all over foxy body peaches cut on "Megan the stallion started dancing and popped another x pill peaches took foxy panties off and ate her Tim told them to let's take this shit to the bedroom? Before leaving peaches turned the music up a notch and lead the way to the room they rushed took off their clothes and got straight to it he was kissing peaches while Goxy was eating her Pussy. Foxy used her free hand to finger her clit until Foxy was soaking wet. That made Tim erect. He put his dick deeply in Foxy and started hitting her in the ass. Foxy kept telling him to fuck her harder. That shit drove peaches insane. She was horny as hell! She told Foxy to climb on her face and ride it. Foxy did what she was told and climbed on top while Tim put his duck in Peaches she put her legs up so he could go deeper

Peaches was sucking Foxy's pussy and she was moaning saying damn Peaches eat my pussy, that feels so good and you got me so wet. Tim was fucking the shit out of her until she was about to climax so he started hitting her faster. The x pill had him fucking the shit out of her he could tell she was eating Foxy's pussy good because she was riding her face at a fast paste. Peaches and Foxy were tired they had busted at least 3 nuts a piece and they fucked for about an hour and fell asleep.

CHAPTER 12

Icy was at Porsha's house talking to her about every detail that involved Biggs the nigga kept texting her phone back to back telling her how he missed her he told her to text Biggs back but she told him baby fuck I'm so horny I'm ready to get some dick we can worry about that shit later. Porsha finished telling him everything that she knew she told him about the alarm code and how he leaves dope and money sitting around Icy told Porsha how he loved her and that once the lick was done he and Levelle would be moving in with her. Porsha told him I heard this sane lit once before so I ain't going to take it to heart. His reply was baby I'm for real I got to start thinking about Levelle I don't want him to grow up like me and Tim ass did. Porsha leaned over and started kissing Icy's dick. She was horny as hell from the x pill that she had popped earlier. She sucked Icy until he was rock-hard. He was playing with her pussy and had her soak and wet. They had sex repeatedly until they fell out. When they were done Porsha walked to the bathroom and ran some bath water. she took a bath texted Biggs a couple of times and headed for the bed. When she got there Icy was knocked out sleep. She started to wake him up but he was sleeping so peacefully. It wasn't until 1:00 pm when they both woke up Icy woke up to 10 missed calls and 3 text messages from Levelle and Tim he checked the two from Levelle first telling him how his head was hurting this morning so he didn't make it home safe and that he already got rid of the car from the shooting. Porsha had 7 missed calls herself 5 of them were from Biggs and the other two were from Peaches telling her that Biggs was looking for her. He even had Dollar calling me all last night. Porsha put her phone back down. She wasn't worried about Biggs. She was happy she had Icy at home with her. She got up, put on her Jimmy Choo robe, and headed toward the kitchen to make breakfast. She knew he wasn't going to lay around all day. The x pills were starting to wear off so she was hungry as hell. She fixed pancakes, sausages, eggs, and two cups of orange juice and placed it on the table. Icy got up stretched and walked to the closet he pulled out his Balmain jumpsuit and a pair of Jordan that matched she kept him brand new boxers, socks, and a toothbrush. Icy placed the clothes on the bed rolled a blunt and headed toward the shower before doing so he walked into the kitchen to give Porsha hug and let her hit the food soon he got in there he said damn this food smells good bae? I'm bout to head in the shower I will eat when I get out her reply was ok kept hitting the bunt and washing dishes.

CHAPTER 13

Levelle and Carlos skipped school to go holla at their homeboy from the hood his name was Lil Fat he told them that he would take them to his OG to buy a gun but it will cost $600. Now Lil Fat was a young nigga getting money. He has been pushing dope since a young age. He was only 17 and had his own car house and kept a fat pocket. Lil fat pulled up at the trap house he told Levelle and Carlos to come inside he asked them did they have the money on them to buy the guns.Levelle's reply was yeah we got it and followed Lil Fat inside the fence they could tell it was a dope house because dope heads were steadily coming in and out. Lil Fat knocked on the door 3 times and a crackhead opened the door to let them in. He told them to sit on the couch while fat was walking toward the back. The inside of the house wasn't so bad for a trap spot it had a fifty-five-inch tv screen on the wall, brown leathery couches and a PlayStation 4 hooked to the tv screen, and a big fish tank that covered the wall. Lil fat came from the back of the house with two baby 40 cabs in his hand. He gave one to Carlos and the other to Levelle. When they looked up he had some black fat nigga following him… I mean jet black. "Black," asked who had the money. Levelle went into his pocket and handed him 600 dollars. He counted it and handed it to the black nigga. He asked them did they need anything else before they leave. He also told them his name was big Sam but everybody called him sam he told them to never pull their guns out unless y'all going to use them. Life is too short and when y'all are ready to make some money out here let me know. I keep the best in town ask Lil Fat. Levelle and Carlos got up gave him a handshake and said thanks big homie and walked out of the house. Lil fat stayed in the house a little longer to get his cut. Remember nobody does shit in the game for free. When Lil fat made it back to the car he drove them back to Carlos's house. Before they could make it Lil fat phone rang none stop it was dope fein trying to buy dope like always he answered the phone took his calls and kept driving he cut the radio down and told them when y'all ready to get done real money let me know I will show y'all the in and outs to this game and plus ain't no sense in skipping school if you nor making money every since I dropped out of school I been getting money so y'all think about it little did he know Levelle and Carlos were on a different mission.Lil fat dropped them off and went back to making his sales. Levelle and Carlos went into the house to check out their new guns. When they took the clip out, the guns were fully loaded. Levelle told Carlos to close the room door so Carlos's mom wouldn't walk up on them…. not that she cared. She was too worried about a crack rock, but Levelle still felt the need to show respect. A lot of times Carlos would get out of line with his mom and want to disrespect her but Levelle wouldn't let him. He always told Carlos you only have one mom! No matter what she do she's still your mom and that's why Carlos loved him. He always kept him on his toes. That's what you call a real nigga. Icy and Porsha had breakfast took a shower and got dressed before leaving icy told Porsha he would call her later before walking out he gave her a hug and a kiss she didn't really want him to leave but she knew he had other things in the streets to take care of.when Icy made it to the car he dialed Tim's number. One thing he always had to do is check on him because he was a live wire and very hot-headed. When he called Tim the phone rang 3 times and he picked up sounding like he was still laying down tired. Icy asked did he get any sleep? Tim's reply was a little not really. Icy reply was if you would've gone home instead of going over Peaches' house you wouldn't be tired. Tim's reply was I'm good. I'm over here with my baby Vasha's ass. You know I had to come see my baby. He trying to make her feel good because she was laying next to him. But everything is good on that other top. I will call you when I wake up a nigga tired. They both laughed and ended the call. After ending the call with Tim, Icy called Levelle's phone. He noticed he had been letting him slide with so much. The phone rang 3 times and went straight to voicemail so icy called the phone right back it ring 2 times and

Levelle answered what's up Unk? Icy asked him where are you ? His reply was still over Levelle's house. Icy reply was get your things ready I will be there in a couple of minutes to pick you up so be outside. They both ended the call. Levelle got off the phone and told Carlos Unk about to come get me and hide my gun I don't need him tripping, you know how that nigga is. He should let me come back if he doesn't I will call you and don't do any crazy shit with these guns bro. Carlos's reply was bro I'm about to call Mena and see if her moms going to work tonight so I might be over there just call my phone. Mena was Carlos's girlfriend her mother worked from three to eleven at night so when he wasn't hanging out with Levelle he was at her house he hated being home I'm plus they had been dating for years he loved her. Icy pulled up and blew the horn so Levelle would come outside on the cool he was mad that Levelle didn't go to school so he had to check him before it became a habit. Carlos abs Levelle walked outside and did their handshake then Levelle got in the car before they could pull off Carlos's mom walked up to the car trying to buy some dope icy told her he didn't have anything on him so he gave her 29 dollars and drove off she knew he didn't sale dope in front of her son and Levelle he asked Levelle was he hungry? his reply was yes I haven't eaten since earlier. Icy pulled up at chicken king restaurant and bought two platters of chicken, waffles, and fries when they got the food they parked in the parking lot abs ate icy ate half of his food he was trying to put something on his stomach so the x pills wouldn't have him feeling bad.

CHAPTER 14

Porsha was on the phone with peaches telling her about the good times she had with icy last night she even told her how he ate her pussy all morning Peaches told her how Tom fucked her and Foxy all night. Porsha's line had beeped it was Biggs calling she thought about not answering but Peaches told her to stop acting like that Porsha gave in and clicked over before she could speak Biggs was telling her how he missed her and how happy he was to hear from her she was pretending like she had been sleeping all day and how she had been overwhelmed with work last night his reply was I understand I had Dollar they both out into laughter she changed the subject asking him as he at home? His reply was yea she told him she would be over once she got out of the shower and they ended the call she clicked back over but Peaches had already hung up. Porsha got dressed she put on her Tommy girl outfit with her air max ten plus to match she put in her body spray and headed out the door before leaving she made sure she didn't have any new jockeys on her neck from last night. The last thing she need was for him to feel like she a hoe and she really liked him a lot but she was in love with Icy ass. But she understood love alone doesn't pay bills. When she pulled up at Biggs house she noticed a grey Benz was parked outside his house. She didn't want to just walk up to the door unannounced in case it was one of his side chicks. The last thing she needed was drama from a nigga. So she sent him a text that read, "I'm outside baby." A couple of minutes later she saw the front door swing open and there stood Biggs in a all white and red Gucci outfit with the shoes to match. He looked like he was about to step in a club or something. When Porsha walked in she noticed there were stacks of money laying all over the table and at least 30 blocks of cocaine. Biggs walked her to the living, fired up a blunt, and handed to her. When Rico saw Porsha his mouth dropped. He was a Mexican that had swag like a black nigga. He was dressed to impress. He had a Fendi outfit on with the shoes and belt to match, he also had three diamond chains on his neck and a bust down Rolex. Biggs told Rico that all the money was there like always and stuffed it all in an LV duffle bag. Truth be told he was trying to rush Rico off. No nigga wants to seem like a worker in front of their woman even tho he had long money. Everyone works for somebody in this game. Rico grabbed the bags off the table and headed toward the door. Before leaving he told Biggs how sexy Porsha was, he even asked her did she have any sisters or friends. Porsha's reply was no sisters but I have a couple of homegirls for you. Rico told Biggs to give her the number and headed out the door. Biggs walked Rico out to the car and went back into the house. Soon as he hit the door he rushed over to Porsha and told her to give him a hug and a kiss. When she got up he squeezed her ass and told her how much he missed her. They sat down on the couch and were smoking a blunt when Biggs phone started ringing back to back. He rejected everyone that was calling because the city was dry with dope. Porsha hit him on the chest and told him to answer for his little females. His reply was that's all money baby, they will wait. I'm the only nigga that got dope right now. After smoking a couple blunts Biggs looks over and asks Porsha was it cool if she goes out of town with him. Her reply was you know I have to work baby. You should have told me and I could have arranged to take off. Plus my boss still tripping from missing work the other day. We can go next weekend if the offer still stands? His reply was you know it's cool bab. Therefore, he could make better plans. He wanted to show off for her and he know the perfect spot he was taking her. Biggs phone kept ringing so he picked up it was a cat name Dirt. He said what up lil bro? Dirt's reply was you tell me... is shit still all good? Biggs's reply was you know that my well doesn't run dry. If you still need that three I will be over in like 15 minutes. Dirt's reply was ok big bro and they ended the call. When Biggs ended the call he rolled up a blunt of exotic weed and asked Porsha if would she ride with him. Her reply was ok baby no problem. He grabbed 3 bricks of coke off the table, put them in a Gucci backpack, and headed toward the door. Before leaving he made sure the alarm was on because he had too much dope in there. On the way to Dirt house, Biggs was bumping "Lil Dirk throughout the speakers. When they pulled up you can tell the city was dry because every nigga that meant something in the city was at the same trap house. I mean it was Bentleys, Audis, and BMWs lined up one behind the other. Biggs took out his phone and called Dirt's phone. Before he could answer Dirt was walking outside within 3 minutes. Dirt walked to the all-white Range Rover and sat in the backseat. Porsha had turned her head quickly because she know him from the strip club. I mean the nigga used to make it rain heavy. Truth be told she got with Dirt like one or two times back but hadn't seen him in a while and he was looking fine as ever. When Dirt got in, he placed a black and brown mcm bag full of cash in the backseat that held $90,000. Biggs gave him the backpack that had the dope inside. Dirt noticed Porsha so he spoke calling her by her real name. That shocked Biggs but he downplayed it like he didn't hear it. Biggs and Dirt did their handshake like always. Before Dirt could get out he told him bro you know I keep the best shit so get at me. Dirt's reply was you know that bro I will call you later. When they pulled off Biggs fired up the blunt and played "Sada baby" loudly out the speaker. Porsha reached over and cut the radio down and her exact words were baby I have something to tell you. The last thing she needed was him to think she was a hoe so she wanted to be honest. You know bae I use to get with Dirt he use to come into the club throw money so I got with him abs haven't seen him until now. Biggs knew she wasn't lien being dirt been locked up in a parole hold abs was sent to prison but beat the charge and was released. His exact words were I respect you for that baby and since we on some keep it real shit let me tell you this... you remember we went out to eat at chili's the waitress chick that kept looking? I use to fuck with her a couple of months back. What he didn't know that was like a slap to the face to her in fact that shit pissed her off even more. There it was she was trying to keep it real and a nigga had been on some fuck shit the whole time. She looked at him and ask so if I wouldn't have told you about Dirt you would've never told me about this bitch? He tried to pass her the blunt but she told him ,no thank you just drop me off. At this point, I hate you because you have shown me that you are a disloyal ass nigga. You took me out to eat and you know your bitch worked there. That let me know if we didn't work out you would do the same thing to me to make me mad. Y'all niggas out of there! Just drop me off please. On the way to the house Biggs had tried to talk to her but she wouldn't reply to anything he was saying. She did say a word until she reached the driveway. He tried to touch her once more but she rejected. Porsha jumped out of the car and left so fast he couldn't do anything but hit his fist on the dashboard. Biggs walked into the house upset he cut off the alarm feeling fucked up here it was everybody was going good but he had fucked that up. He kept trying to call her phone but she kept sending him to voicemail back to backbit still no answer. Porsha called Peaches phone to tell her the tea about what just happened between her and Biggs soon as peaches picked up Porsha got straight down to business Peaches heard her out but didn't say a word until Porsha was completely finished talking. Porsha keep talking until she noticed her best friend hadn't said a word she ask Peaches bitch why are you so quite today? Her reply was bitch you already know not to be playing games with these dog ass niggas and secondly, he don't owe you any loyalty you act like you been fucking with this nigga bitch y'all just met Porsha cut her off and told her bitch you right but how would you feel if a Biggs took you some were that his old bitch worked at? Peaches reply was yea you're right girl that was some foul ass shit but now you know how to handle his ass drain his pockets you know he going to keep blowing your phone up so duck his ass for about a week if he shows up at the club cuss his ass the fuck out then he will get the memo. Porsha's line kept beeping so she told her best friend she will call her back matter of fact bitch don't go nowhere and ended the call.

CHAPTER 15

Tim woke up at Vasha's house she had left to run to chicken king to get the wings she had just ordered she didn't want to wake Tim because he was sleeping so peacefully I'm plus she wasn't ready for him to leave yet. Tim walked into the shower and turned it on he heard Vasha come into the house he started to go in there but thought against it because he know she was ready to have more sex and he was ready to hit the streets. Tim cut the water off dried off and put his clothes on when he was done he put his clothes on and headed toward the kitchen when he made it his plate was set neatly on the table he told her thanks bae and ate his food while doing so he powered his phone on to check his text messages luckily no one important had called just a couple messages from Foxy telling him how she enjoyed him last night he read the messages and start smiling. He finished his food got up gave Vasha a hug and a kiss he told her he would call her later her reply was baby make me a promise that you will come back later? and be careful on these streets? I will hate to see you locked up baby. Tim gave her another kiss and walked out the door. When Tim left Vasha cleaned up and put on a movie she was trying to enjoy her day off until her phone started ringing she was hoping it was Tim's ass but when she looked at the screen she saw her boss's name flash she started not to answer but she picked up trying to sound tired his exact words were sorry to bother you but I need a favor? I need you to work overtime on this case it's too high profile her reply was okay sounding dry but knew he wasn't taking no for an answer he said a quick joke like always and ended the call. Tim went straight to the house to change clothes he had already showered over at Vasha's house but didn't keep changing clothes there because when they were into it she would bleach all his shit. Tom walked into the house to find Levelle and Icy playing the game he was glad to see Levelle badass he didn't have any kids so he had super love for him plus he had been raising Levelle ever since his mother died. Tim walked into the room put on his Balmain outfit with a pair of Jordan's then he went sat on the couch next to Levelle he was still hung over and tired but he was cool Levelle had beaten Icy on the game three times back to back that little nigga was a beast when it came down to that video game for real. Icy phone rang and he saw Porsha's name flash across the screen. He was glad she called because he need Levelle to stay over at her house so he would make it to school tomorrow. Icy answered hello baby how are you doing? She said hello baby wyd his reply nothing at the house getting my ass kicked in the game by Levelle by the way I need him to come stay a night with you so he can go to school his badass has been out too many days already. Her reply was, now come on baby he can stay anytime. Bring him before I go to work so I can get up and drop him off. His reply was okay baby. I might stay over myself I'm bout to get him ready and we will be over. Her reply was ok bae, and they ended the call. When the call ended he told Levelle to pack an overnight bag he was staying over at Porsha's house so she would make sure he get to school. His reply was okay. He was happy Porsha always looked out for him and she was cool as hell and gave him money.

CHAPTER 16

Trae Trae and his click were riding with their guns drawn in hand they were looking for Icy and Tim for robbing him he had already paid Ron Ron and his brothers to shoot up Icy and Tim's house now somebody killed them they already got the call it was Icy and Tim was the ones responsible for the murders and plus Ron Ron them was his favorite cousins. He still couldn't believe that they got caught slipping and didn't at least get a chance to shoot back. Lil Red was calling Trae Trae's phone back to back trying to tell him where Tim's apt was but he didn't answer so she shoot him a text message and left a voicemail as well. Trae Trae was riding around and noticed his phone was steady ring back to back so he picked it up and saw Lil red name flashing he wasn't trying to answer until Icy and Tim were dead he knew he was the reason they were dead. He looked down at his text messages and saw nothing but texts from Lil red when he read the messages he hurried up and failed her number the phone rang 1 time and she picked up he told Steele to cut the radio down real quick this my lil cousin she know we're these fuck niggas hiding at. Lil red was crying soon as she picked up the phone she was saying something but you couldn't understand her due to the crying Trae Trae's exact words were calm down cousin I know you hurt we all are but we got to be strong for them believe me I won't stop lurking these streets until them niggas are dead she cut him off I told you I know we're they stay just come get me you know I use to fuck with Tim do pick me up I will show you were his apt at. Trae Trae's reply was I will be over in a couple of minutes be outside because I don't even want to look at aunt Carlin right now her reply was I know cuz but she needs you just step in for a second then we can leave his reply was say less I will be there in a minute and ended the call. When the call ended he told Steele to go by aunt Carlin's house Lil red just called and said she got the drop in them niggas they already had crossed a line when they robbed me but now they killed my little cousins.

CHAPTER 17

Levelle was calling Carlos's phone to tell him that he wasn't coming back over to his house and that he was staying at Porsha but he wasn't answering the phone the last two times so he called back a third time and Carlos picked up on the first ring. Carlos's exact words were what up bro? He sounded like he was sleeping Levelle reply was, what the hell you be doing I been calling you? Carlos's reply was nothing, I just woke up I just left Megan's house. I told you I was going over there for a while. You know she drained my ass! They both started laughing. Levelle broke the silence… did you put the guns up before you left home? Carlos's reply was yea I put them up and I'm walking through the door now. You know I can't leave shit laying around because momma will sell that shit to get high. I hate my momma out here smoking dope and we barely have food in the house. Plus she sells all the food stamps. Levelle's reply was, stay strong bro we going to make shit happen we just need to get at Lil fat ass but I will call you in the morning, and don't bring me any clothes. Unk gave me a robin outfit. Carlos's reply was okay bro and tell Porsha sexy ass I said hey. Carlos got off the phone and went into the kitchen trying to find something to eat. After looking, all he could find was hamburger meat. He took it down, seasoned it, and started cooking. While cooking he heard music coming from his mom's bedroom. He also heard a lot of voices which was normal... his mom always had people over like it was a club or something. He walked down to his mom's room and went in to see at least 5 crackheads with their pipes fired up. What hurt the most is to see his mom hit the pipe in front of him. He slammed the door and went back to check on his food. He was mad, hurt, and frustrated with life. I mean he had been around crackheads his whole life but never knew how to sell it but Lil fat had already told them he would show them the ropes. He went into the room ate the burger and fries and listened to rap music on his phone for about 30 mins. The whole time he was thinking of calling Lil fat but one thing he hated was asking anyone for help. He was in deep thought until he heard someone knocking on the front door. He walked to the door gun drown in hand. He knew his mom couldn't hear the door because of the music. Soon as he opened the door there stood a cat named Rip. He was known from the hood for selling bricks of cocaine. Rip asked Carlos was his mom there. His reply was yeah she's in there like always. Go knock on her door I'm sure she waiting like always. Before Rip went into the back room he reached into his pocket and told Carlos here's 40 dollars, spend it wisely. He gave Carlos his number and headed toward the back room. Carlos went back into his room took, out his phone, and called Lil fat number. The phone ring 3 times and he picks up saying what up lil bro? Carlos replies yeah I'm just thinking and chilling man. I need to make some money. It's so many dope fiends running in and out of my house, I could be making that money. Lil fat reply was ok I feel you, bro, I will come to get you tomorrow and show you the ins and outs of this shit. His reply was okay I will call you after school bro and they ended the call.

CHAPTER 18

Peaches was at home chilling listening to music she looked in her purse and noticed she didn't have any more weed so she called her weed man he picked straight up like always what up baby? Nothing need some of that fire-ass weed you had if you are around? His reply was I'm around the corner so bring out fine add outside and ended the call. Mon pulled up outside Peaches house just to see her standing on the porch looking sexy as ever she came outside wearing nothing but done bitty shorts and a sports bra soon as she got in she handed him 59 dollars while he weighed the OG kush he looked over at her and asked why she always got to play him? Her reply was you say the same thing every time you pull up. like I tell you every time, come on with that cash I got you. I buy weed from you to support your hustle but you never come to the club to support mine. He looked over at her and say you know I be in these streets trying to eat, but I will come through the club this weekend to support you. know this Benz I'm pushing ain't cheap and I just had a little girl last week so I been on my grind lately. Peaches look over at Mon and said I feel you on that! Hell, my bills ain't cheap, but congratulations on your baby. Here go an extra 40 dollars buy the baby something. Now when you are ready to fuck with a real grown woman call me, and I will only charge you $200. Before she could get out of the car he told her he would hit her up later on. Before he could say anything else her phone started to ring. He looked at the screen and noticed Porsha's name she picked up saying what yo bitch? Porsha's reply was I'm outside your house pulling up so come outside bitch. Peaches reply was I'm outside getting done weed from Mon young ass she heard Mon mumble something but she didn't know what he said she hung up the phone and asked him what he said? His reply was like I said ain't nothing young about me. She couldn't lie Mon was fine ass hell karma light brown eyes with dreads that hung to the middle of his back and the had the best weed in the city so if he wanted to act grown she was going to rock his world he was on 21 years of age so she knew he ain't had no grown woman in his life and she planned on doing just that she looked at him and said I will call you after work just answer the phone. When she got out of the car Porsha was pulling up and parking her car so she waved her inside it was really chilly outside abs she was ready to get inside the house. Once they were inside peaches cut on the radio and rolled a couple of blunts. She asked Porsha what did she want to drink? Her reply was Hennessy bitch you know that girl! I'm so glad that nigga Biggs done stopped blowing up my phone back to back. I just got off the phone with Icy, he bring Levelle over so I can take his ass to school. I bet he ain't been in days their sister will flip in her grave if she knew that they ass been out here doing all this shit. Peaches looked over at Porsha and started laughing girl let me find out you playing step momma? Peaches rolled up another blunt and told Porsha I know it's going to be jumping in the club tonight at work it's Thursday and I got to pay my rent care note girl I wish I had a nigga to give me 1,000 dollars just to look pretty you always catch the ballers Porsha reply was girl fuck Biggs dog ass don't even speak that nigga ass up. They smoked a couple of blunts and rapped Sada Baby for the next hour until Porsha's phone started to ring she saw the name Icy flashed across the screen so she picked up baby how are you doing? His reply ok I'm about to bring Levelle over there so meet me there and the call ended. When she got off the phone she told peaches she would see her at work tonight. Peaches reply was be careful you know your ass can barely drive when you drink. Porsha's reply was girl I'm good, now let me go see my man. Peaches reply was, shut up! You see Icy ass every day and tell his ass to tell my man to come home tonight.

CHAPTER 19

Biggs was at home rolling blunts he had just woken up to 20 missed calls most of them were from this cat from Memphis name Flex. He came down every two weeks to get 10 keys of coke. he was glad Flex had woken him up because missing his calls was bad for business. He had at least 5 missed calls from Trina a couple of calls from Dollar but none from Porsha she hasn't called one time. Biggs dialed Flex's phone back it rings 3 times and picks up. What it do bro I been calling? Biggs reply was I was sleeping bro my bad but where are you? Flex's reply was at the mall but I will meet you at our little spot. Biggs's reply was I will be there in 20 minutes. Flex's reply was ok I'm waiting and ended the call. When Biggs got off the phone with Flex he dial Dollar up it rings 3 times. He picked up sounding like he was still sleeping. What it do nigga? Biggs reply was nothing get your ass up where you at? His reply was at the house. I got the money for them two bricks. I hope shit back good, because the whole city blowing my phone up. Biggs reply was yea shit good! I will be over there in 45 minutes, I got to go handle something. Flex down here and he been waiting. I overslept. Dollar's reply was okay I will be waiting on you and they ended the call.

CHAPTER 20

Trae Trae and his chick had pulled up at Lil Red's house. It was jammed pack with cars. You could hear the music playing from the streets and could hear them talking loud inside the house. He told his boys to stay in the car and keep their eyes open. He just needed to pay his respects to aunt Carlin before he end up dead or in prison. Steele's reply was okay we going to hold it down. TJ and Lil Mack didn't say a word they just sat back snorting their coke. They were known for killing. They were from Chicago but Trae Trae had sent for them after he got robbed at the club by Icy and Tim. He knows if he would have sent them Icy and Tim ass would be dead but Ron Ron kept begging to kill them for how Tim treated their sister. As Trae Trae got out of the car he was calling Lil Red's number. She picked straight up but he couldn't hear anything she was saying because the background was too loud to hear. He spoke louder on the phone and told her to come outside. Before he could say anything else Lil Red was walking on the porch. Soon as she made it to him she hugged him and broke down crying. Her exact words were cuz I can't believe them niggas killed my brother! His reply was, don't worry them niggas gone die on my daughter now let's go in here so I can holla at your mom's. When they walked in everyone was drinking, playing cards, and dominos Aunt Carlin was in her room looking at Ron Ron, Lil Dave, Dirt, and Lil Steve pictures crying and praying at the same time. Lil Red went hugged her and told her mom everything would be ok Carlin looked up and saw Trae Trae her favorite lil nephew so she wiped her face and told him boy bring your ass over here and give me a hug. You look just like your daddy. I remember I use to beat your ass… his reply was yea I remember I use to want to stay over here every weekend and you use to make everybody in the house go to church. I hate to see you hurt like this auntie here go $5,000. I will bring you more tomorrow. I love you and be strong for me. Her reply was Trae Trae be careful out there I would have a fit if something happened to you. I already know you going to retaliate but please be careful because this family can't take to no more losses. Trae Trae's reply was ok aunt I will and he walked out of the room before she saw the tears that were falling from his face. When he left out the room Lil Red waved him over to talk to some lady name Jackie. He spoke and Lil Red said this is Ron Ron girls mom you could see the hurt in her eyes her eyes were swollen and had bags underneath them he also hugged her and told her everything would be ok I will find them niggas who did this to your daughters her reply was don't worry about it baby the lord going to fix it Mrs. Jackie looked at Lil Red and asked her who is this handsome boy? Her reply was Jackie this is uncle Trae's son that's lil Trae you remember him soon as she hear the name she jumped up boy I remember you come here and give me another hug I remember me and your daddy used to be lovers back in the days you look just like him when he was your age tell him he better come see me when he makes it to town ok? Trae's reply was I will tell him he said he will be here Saturday her reply was ok and went back to playing cards. Trae Trae felt bad for getting his lil cousins killed he knew if it wasn't for him sending them over Icy and Tim's house they would be still living to this day but he wasn't going to let anybody know not even Lil Red he know for sure she loved her brothers and would be hurt if she found out he was responsible for her brothers' death. Trae Trae and Lil Red walked out of the house and headed to the car he let her get in the front seat because Lil Mack and TJ were in the back the last thing he needed was for them to smart off to her and she gets to talking recklessly at the mouth. Icy, Tim and Levelle walked out of the house and got in the car. On the way to Porsha's house, Icy asked Levelle was he hungry. His reply was yes I haven't eaten since earlier. Icy didn't want him to go over there hungry because he didn't have time to hear Porsha's mouth about why haven't I fed him. Icy looked in the back seat and asked Levelle did you get the outfit out of the closet? His reply was yes it's in my bag. Icy bumped Tim and told him to look at this lil nigga trying to go to school all fly and shit. Levelle loved when his uncles let him were their clothes. They wore the same size and plus they wore nothing but the best. They pulled up at Ralls, got something to eat, and headed toward Porsha's house. When they pulled up to her house she was sitting in the car listening to slow music. Tim looks at Icy and started laughing. His exact words were boy you are a head hunter. You got her sitting outside waiting on your ass. Everyone in the car started laughing. Porsha got out of the car gave Icy a kiss and Levelle a hug. She told them to come inside and get comfortable. She got their plastic plates and sat them on the table. One thing about her is she doesn't play about her apt. Tim looked up at her and said girl we don't need no plates, ole bougie ass. We ain't going to drop shit on your carpet. Her reply was fuck you, I was trying to help y'all out. You always got to talk shit. Don't make me call my girl on your ass. His reply was she knows I'm the king and started laughing. Porsha told Icy to come to the room. He walked to the room and sat on the bed. Porsha shut the door and went kissed him. She sat next to him rolled a blunt and cut in the stereo. Icy ate his food while Porsha searched for an outfit to were for tonight for the strip club. She took out her lotion, perfume, and a black strip suit and sat it on the bed. Icy was done eating his food he took the blunt and fired it up he hit the blunt 3 times and was choking none stop. He asked Porsha what kind of weed was this. Her reply was Runtz bae. I got some in my purse I got it from Biggs. She leaned over to get the weed, he slid his hand up her dress, she hit his hand and told him to stop unless he was ready to fuck her. His reply was, I will be later bae and licked his lips. She was smiling from ear to ear. Tim was in the front room talking to Levell. He was telling him in the next week or two we going to buy you a car and how he wished his mom was still living. Shit hasn't been the same ever since she been gone but don't worry we got you. Just stay strong and stay in school. Levelle was about to say something else until Icy walked in there and told Tim they had a run to make. Before leaving they hugged him and walked out the door.

CHAPTER 21

Biggs made it home, went inside, and cut the alarm off. When he made it inside he forgot to pick up Trina so he shot her a text.... bae I forgot to come get you but I'm at home. Her reply was on my way daddy be there in ten minutes. Biggs called Dollar's phone a couple of times and he picked straight up. What it do bro? Dollar's reply was I'm outside, unlock the door. Biggs got up, unlocked the door, and sat back down at the table. He was rolling blunts of the exotic weed he had got. He always rolled a couple of blunts. His phone started ringing and he didn't have time. Dollar walked into the house with a black Prada duffel bag. He sat it on the table and pulled out the $60,000 that he owed Biggs for the two bricks he fronted him. They did their handshake and kept talking. Dollar looked at Biggs and told him, bro I'm going to need 5 bricks this time. The whole city calling me! Biggs reply was, bro, get you 5 off the table and my phone has been blowing up too. Hell yeah, that nigga Flex told me to tell you what's up. That nigga bought a trucking company and has a baby on the way. I'm thinking about buying myself something. This dope game doesn't last forever hell

I have to make an exit plan. Dollar's reply was hell yea bro this shit doesn't last forever. I got $350,000 saved but that ain't shit but it's better to have and don't need rather than need and don't have. I remember times we could barely pay our rent now we own our house. Biggs reply was hell yeah I just wish wifey and the kids were here. Ain't shit like family! Dollar's reply was I understand you have to stay strong. Have you talked to Porsha? Trying to change the subject. Biggs reply was fuck her! I'm a boss! She will call me before I call her! Dollar replied now that's the Biggs I know. Don't ever let no female make you feel like you need them! You have been in these streets plus you could buy 100 females. Dollar brought up Trina to dead the conversation and Porsha. Biggs reply speaking of her, she about to pull up right now and I'm about to fuck the shit out of her! They started laughing until Dollar's phone rang. He picked up what up lil bro? Rex replied nothing, we been waiting on you for 2 hours you still coming? Dollar's reply was yea on the way now. I'm over her hollering at Biggs now. Rex's reply was tell big homie I said what's up. Tell him to let me drive the Bentley this weekend. Dollar's reply was ok I will tell him, I'm on my way now and ended the call. Dollar grabbed 5 bricks off the table and put them in his Prada bag. He told Biggs he would hit him later and headed towards the door. Before he could open it somebody was knocking at the door. Dollar opened the door and it was Trina standing there looking like a baby about to get some candy. She walked right past him. She knew he would say something smart like always he could do nothing but laugh dollar told Biggs to lock the door and headed toward his car.

CHAPTER 22

Icy and Tim were riding around smoking and drinking like always they we're talking about Levelle and how they had to make sure he was good all they could do is think about their big sister they missed her so much she was always fussing like she was their mom but she kept the family on point. Icy told time to ride by the house so he could get his money he was ready to hit the strip club again before they could make it to the house Icy phone began to ring it was an old school nigga name Killer every time he calls he need 2 or 3 zips of coke they sold coke from time to time but mostly robbed icy picked up the phone what's good bro? Killer reply I need 4 zips this time so come through real fast? Icy reply was I will be over soon and ended the call. When he hung up Icy looked at Tim and said that was that nigga killer he needs 4 zips so hurry up we can't miss that sale. Tim's reply was shut up nigga what you want me to fly? Trae Trae and Lil Red them were outside were sitting outside Icy and Tim's apt Lil Mack and TJ were snorting coke ready to put the murder game down they had been sitting outside in the car waiting for about an hour but Icy and Tim still haven't shown up. Lil Ted was the first to speak I know them niggas going to pull up soon this is where they stay before she could say another word Tim and Icy were pulling up she Pinter at the car and said that's them right there. Trae Trae asked everyone if were they ready and on point. Steele's reply was we've been ready Trae Trae told Lil Red to stay in the car the last thing he needed was her getting shot. When the car pulled in everybody jumped out with their guns drown shoots rung out everywhere Tim hit the gas and the car hit the trash can glads flew everywhere Trae Trae emptied his whole clip while Lil Mack and TJ kept shooting until they saw the passenger door swing open Lil Red saw Icy get out the car so she began to scream come on y'all somebody getting out the car everybody made it to the car trying to get in but Icy was right in their tracks shooting Steele put the car in drive but Icy wasn't letting up he was letting his gun rip Trae Trae abs Lil Mack had got shot Lil Red was hollering Steele go what the fuck you waiting on he almost hit a parked car but managed to straight the wheel Lil Red cut in the light and saw blood coming from Lil Mack and Trae Trae bleeding she panicked and told Steele to go straight to the hospital he was doing 100 mph trying to get to the hospital TJ was holding Lil Mack crying Trae Trae was holding his side Steele was trying to calm everybody down but the scene was Chios. Steele pulled up to the hospital ten mins later and parked at the front door he told Lil Ref to help Tj carry Lil Mack in the hospital while he rushed and helped Trae Trae. When they made it inside nurses were screaming it was blood everywhere they put Lil Mack on the stretcher while the other nurses gave Trae Trae a wheelchair two police ran from the back to help from the looks of it Lil Mack want going to make it. Steele grabbed Lil Red and told her to stay there and don't tell the police shit. Her reply was I ain't saying shit now hurry up and leave before the police come out looking for the car. His reply was ok and ran out of the hospital. Icy was trying to get Tim out of the car. It was blood everywhere. He tried to start the car but it wouldn't start. Tim was shot in the arm and stomach. He was bleeding bad and and and Icy was shot in the arm. He was searching for his phone... he could believe he had just gotten caught slipping. Icy phone was steadily ringing. It was Porsha calling. Icy answered sounding like he was in a rage. He asked Porsha where the fuck you at? Her reply on my way to work bae what's wrong? His reply was Tim just got shot hurry up and come before the police come and ended the call. Luckily the neighbors were outside they waved at Icy and told him to calm down. Then a guy walked up and told Icy let me help you out bro, we heard the shooting. It sounded like thunder! Icy reply was, yeah, some niggas came through shooting. Icy grabbed Tim and told him to hold on everything would be ok. Tim was so weak he couldn't speak. His forehead was sweating and his arm was limp. The guy that was helping Icy told him to bring Tim inside. He gave him a towel and told him to place it

PLAY NO GAMES MAKE NO MISTAKES

on Tim's head. Icy grabbed Tim's gun off him shit happened so fast that Tim didn't get to get a shot off. Icy couldn't do anything but cry the thought of Tim dying gutted him like hell the neighbor was so cool he told Icy to give him the guns he would put them up police cars see pulling up everywhere. Porsha was speeding over to Tim's house she was crying and running stop signs. she called Peaches phone and it went to voicemail. she called back and Peaches picked up on the second ring. Porsha was hollering on the phone, bitch icy and Tim just got shot meet me at the hospital! Peaches reply was I'm on my way now and ended the call. Porsha pulled up at Tim's house and saw police cars everywhere and an ambulance. the whole apartment was tapped off so she put her car in park and walked toward the crime scene until she was stopped by the police officer I'm sorry we can't let you in so please stay back. Porsha was crying so hard she could barely talk Icy heard the commotion and stuck his head out baby please just meet us at the hospital? Her reply was okay bae on my way just hang in there. Porsha ran every red light in sure until she reached the hospital. Detective Chris pulled up to the apartment and jumped out of his car he was at home chilling until he heard icy and Tim nabe run across the scanners so he rushed to the scene. When icy saw Chris's face he put his head down he knew it was going to be a long night he wasn't so much worrying bout jail he was more worried about Tim was in the ambulance going in and out that was the last thing he remembers next thing he knew he was awakened by two police officers and a nurse standing over him. due to all the pain, he could barely talk. When the police saw his eyes open he got on his phone and said a couple of words and detectives rushed in everywhere. they were trying to ask him questions but the doctor requested that Tim be left alone it's standard procedure for a doctor to do while the patient was under their care Tim was unresponsive and needed time to heal. The detectives left a card and told the nurse to call soon as he was awake then left the room. The doctor was an older black lady who looked like she was in her late 40s and had a heart of gold her hair hind the middle of her back and her eyes were grey she understood how it felt to be shot. The doctor told Tim not to worry because she had a son that died he had got shot 3 years ago from being shoot and robbed by his best friend she never liked her son best friend Travis he always seemed jealous of her son Susan she remember one time Susan and his older brother broke into Susan apt awhile back thinking he had drugs in there but little did they know I kept all the real dope at my house. My son was doing good until one day I got a call saying he was unresponsive and shot up badly when I got there I broke down all the nurses said he just came out of a coma and the punk ass detectives kept pressing him to talk until his blood pressure ran up abs he died from that day forth she promised to protect any patient and let them recover before questioning. Doctor Wallace told Tim to lay back and relax she told him that he had been shot pretty badly but the surgery went well. she also told Tim that his brother had been shot in the arm but he would be released in a few because it was an in-and-out shot. Tim was trying to say something but the pain was too unbearable. the Doctor told him to lay back, she would give him a notebook and pen to write on. His exact words were to tell my brother not to tell the police anything and tell him to contact Vasha ASAP then he laid back on the hospital bed he didn't know if he could trust her but that's the chance he had to take. Doctor Wallace read the note and rushed out of the room trying to catch his brother Icy before the hospital release him. When she made it to his room she noticed the same detectives from earlier were standing there talking to Icy. She walked into the room and asked everyone were they ok? Detectives Williams's reply was yes we just need a minute to talk to this client her reply was ok I will be back to check on the client in 10 minutes. On her way down the hallway she saw two more detectives approaching she wasn't worried about Icy telling, she could tell he respect the street code. When she walked into the room she heard the detectives asking Icy what he saw. His reply was fuck you pigs I ain't got shit to say. Vasha and Chris walked into the room they told the two rookies detectives that they were taking over the case matter of fact y'all go check on the other victims that are sitting in the waiting room then meet us back at the station. The two detectives were heading

99

to Trae Trae's room but they were approached by the hospital security he told them that it was two people sitting in the wades area they were the ones who bought the victim here the detectives told the security thanks for the info and headed toward the lobby. Levelle Thomas aka Lil Mack was still in surgery the doctors were doing everything to help him fight for his life while Trae Trae was doing good and barely in pain all he can think about is his cousins that just died and his little girl that he loved dearly. The detectives walked up to Lil Red and TJ they didn't even notice the detectives because Lil Red was crying and TJ was holding her telling her everything would be ok and how everybody gone die behind this. Detective Oliver grabbed Lil Red by the shoulder to embrace her the only words she could tell her is I know you hurts but you can't fight this battle on your own we need to get statements from y'all I need y'all to follow us to the station ok? Lil Red's reply was it would be a waste of time we didn't see anything detectives I just lost 4 brothers and now my cousin in her fighting I'm going through too much she tried to say something else but she broke down crying again TJ looked the detectives and told them straight up don't you think she is going through a lot? Detectives Williams's reply was I understand y'all are hurting but right now y'all are involved in a crime scene so either we can do it the hard way or the easy way now the security is back there running the tape to see who the person who drooped y'all off soon as we get the tape his face will be placed all over the newspaper the car y'all was police evidence.Detectives Williams walked away to call the lead detectives he didn't know what to do it wasn't like Lil Red or TJ was arrested so by law they didn't have to come to the station but they didn't know that the phone rang two times and Chris picked up hello Chris speaking all yes sir this detectives Williams we were downstairs interviewing the lobby but they claim to not see anything the other victims are in surgery and one is getting stitched up but what I'm calling for the security guard stopped me and told me there were to people in the parking lot that was involved in the shooting he at the car they arrived in was shot up pretty bad they are preparing the tape as we speak I'm trying to find out who was the driver of the car. Detective Chris told him don't let them leave we need them at the station somebody going to crack detectives Williams's reply was ok see you at the station and ended the call.The detective walked back over we're to TJ and Lil Red he told them he had an order from his boss not to let them y'all leave so Unless you want the whole police force out here Lil Red was the first to speak ok I told y'all I don't know anything at least let me see my cousin before we leave or get an update on their status detective Oliver gave it to them raw abs uncut Terrance going to make but till Mack as y'all call him might not make it.TJ snapped naw that's my brother y'all have to let me see him he was flipping over the hospital chairs and everything he could get his hands on the detectives grabbed him try to calm him but he was out of control they put the handcuffs on him. On the way to the car, both detectives were asking questions about where the shooting take place. Who was the guy who dropped y'all off at the hospital? Neither Lil Red nor TJ said a word the whole ride there. When they got out of the car at the police station Tj told Lil red to stay solid everything will play out. Icy had gotten his arm wrapped up. the injury was non-threatening so the doctor would be releasing him. Porsha and Peaches were right on the doctor's heels trying to make sure Icy was ok when she saw his face she ran and gave him a hug and a kiss she didn't give a dam about him being shot she was glad he was alive. Doctor Wallace asked everyone could they step outside while she have a moment with the client including the detectives. Detective Vasha abs Chris left the room with Porsha and peaches right on their heels so as the door was shut the doctor closed the curtain abs held up her finger and told him to be quiet she then handed him a note from his brother Tim he read the note and asked what room was he in? Her reply was 393 now he ok don't go get yourself in trouble the surgery went well let god handle it now make sure you clean this womb twice a day and I gave you perk 10s to help with your pain. Icy told Mrs. Wallace thank you for everything gave her 500 dollars and walked out of the room. When Icy walked out of the room the two detectives were talking and reviewing pics. Soon as they saw him they held up the pics trying to

PLAY NO GAMES MAKE NO MISTAKES

rush him with questions. Icy reply was I don't know them nor who shot me. Detective Chris cut in y'all keep living by this street code shit y'all going to end up dead y'all youngsters think shooting y'all gun back and forward resolve anything until y'all dead or in prison. Icy stepped to Chris now I never gave you any disrespect so miss me with the bull shit and hell yea we live by the street code nigga and next time you disrespect me you will see the detective pushed Tom so Vasha broke it up she told icy to calm down and told Chris to go take terrace statement aka Trae Trae and that's an order. When Chris was out of eyesight Icy told Vasha to let's go see Bri the doctor gave me a note he wrote and he was asking about you her reply was I told him don't leave the house anyways but y'all never listen. She also told time did far no one has said anything the boy Levelle is in surgery he might not make it Icy snapped I don't care who was in that car all of them should have been dead. Matter of fact who was all in that car? Trae Trae from the west side Lil Red Tim ex bitch some guy name TJ and we don't know who else but we reviewing to see who the driver was. They walked into Tim's room and Vasha broke down crying. He had a tube in his throat and his arm was wrapped she was so busy crying she didn't even notice peaches at the end of his bed rubbing his hand. Icy told Vasha please calm down he going to be okay she ran to the bathroom to get herself together she grabbed a towel and wiped her face she was trying to be strong. Vasha walked out of the restroom and stood by Tim. Icy was holding his hand telling him to be strong. We have been through worst so pull through bro now I'm about to go get cleaned up I will be back I love you Icy felt tears coming from his eyes seeing his brother like that messed with his mind. Vasha told Icy to go home and take a shower and try to get some rest I'm not going anywhere no time soon Icy reply was can you step in the hallway I need to speak with you when they hit you the hallway his exact words were sis you got a job to do you know I got bro you know Chris trying to find anything to take your spot. Her reply was fuck that job that's my man and I'm not leaving his side at this point he knew he couldn't talk her out of it he just hugged her and walked back into the room. Icy walked into the room and kissed Tim on the forehead he told Porsha and peaches to come on it was time to get some rest. Detective Chris was still at Trae Trae's room trying to get him to snitch he was steadily showing him pictures of Icy and Tim but he was steadily telling Chris he didn't see the shooter. Chris was screaming so loud at Trae Trae the nurses rushed in asking was everything ok? Trae Trae said no it's not I'm under medical and he keeps trying to question me can you please ask him to leave? The nurses asked detective Chris to speak with him in the hall. When they made it to the hallway the nurses explained the policy to the detective and told him to come back later or put restraints on the patient but she can't keep having people talking loud in the hospital. His reply was ok and thanks a lot.

CHAPTER 23

Icy Porsha and Peaches walked out of the hospital mad sad and devastated at Tims's condition. Porsha told peaches to explain the situation to their boss Ron because she wasn't coming to work tonight. Peaches reply was I got you girl. I might not make it's 1 o'clock and you know he be talking shit but y'all be careful. Icy got in the car without saying a word. Peaches knew he didn't care for her but it was cool with her. Icy looked at his phone and noticed he had missed calls from OX and killer and a lot of numbers he didn't recognize he called ox number first he knew they were worried about them Ox's phone rings 2 times Icy picked straight up what up bro I already heard what happened you know this game is a thinking game one wrong move can have you in prison for life so come on by the house Icy reply was ok I'm on my way and ended the call. When Icy got off the phone he noticed Porsha was crying he asked her what's wrong. Her reply it just hurt me to see Tim hurt like that I need you to come home fuck these streets I wouldn't know what to do if I lose you I got like $20,000 stashed if you need it you can have it he considered chilling but his brother was laying

PLAY NO GAMES MAKE NO MISTAKES

in a hospital bed shit was too deep. He looks over at Porsha and explained bae we did know nobody was waiting outside trying to kill us that bitch Lil Red Trae Trae and them other niggas going to pay her reply was bae that's what scare me I just hope she doesn't tell on y'all I heard the detectives talking her and some other boy is at the station right now his reply was everything going to be ok bae now stop by Ox house I need to holla at him. When they pulled up at Ox house he was sitting outside Icy got out of the car limping Ox helped him into the porch when he sat down Icy ran everything that happened down to OX not leaving out no detail he even told him about the six people that they just killed Ox exact words were you know the rules to the game after y'all went with y'all move y'all should have laid low and what made y'all go to the same apt and y'all just killed the girl brother! Y'all have to think! Honestly, he couldn't answer but he spoke anyways we did know that Trae Trae be with Lil red and for sure we didn't know that nobody would think that we did the shit we fucked up on this shit now it's all coming back to me Trae Trae must have sent Lil Red brothers to come shoot up our house I'm plus Lil Red mad because Tim smacked her up for going in his pocket so that's who showed them niggas our duck out trifling bitch. Ox's reply was hell yeah that bitch got to die I just hope she doesn't put the police in it bitches don't keep it street like niggas so think about your next move did y'all get rid of them guns? Icy reply was yea speaking on that I need a heat Ox reply was here take this 40 cab and I will call you tomorrow so get some rest. Icy reply was I'm going home now and Tim room number 303 in case you want to go out there. Icy got in the car and noticed Porsha on Facebook being nosy like always girls and that dam Facebook will get them killed she didn't even notice him walking back to the car

CHAPTER 24

Biggs was at home chilling smoking a blunt with Trina they had sex serval times now he was watching queen and slim he was in deep thought about his wife she was a real rider she was with him through thick and thin all he could think about is an exit plan and what business would he buy if he left the game? His thoughts were interrupted by Trina she came and sat next to him wrapped her arms around him and told him how much she missed him and how she will always love him his reply was dry I miss you too bae and love you as well I just hate when you complain I'm a businessman I have to worry about making it home safe these streets don't love anybody. Trina cut him off baby I'm working to get my own business and I just be worried about you no mother man has made me feel like you his reply was I understand that baby you just have to learn how to okay your role I just be scared to love abs get close to anybody I lost my wife and kids that took a big part of me just be patient with me everything will work out. Vasha was sitting next to Tim rubbing his hand when detectives Chris walked in he knew how she felt about Tim she told him plenty of times that's why he hated Tim hear it was the woman of his dreams willing to loos her life for a no-good drug dealer that's the main reason Chris gave Tim a hard time he knew vasha was willing to put her job on the line he walked up to vasha and asked her was everything ok? Her reply was yea he's okay the doctors said he will pull through but he hasn't woke up ever since I been here Chris looks down at Vasha and told her you're a strong person at times too strong don't let this situation get you off balance I'm about to head to the station to try to get some leads from the people that brought the gang bangers to the hospital vasha reply was ok to call me and let me know what's going on. Chris walked into the station and noticed Lil Red and sitting in two different integration rooms. He asked the detective have anyone questioned them on the shooting. And did anyone get the security footage from the hospital? Detective Williams's reply was I have the tape and we tried talking to them neither would talk to us.Chris rubbed his hand together while detective Williams hit play in the tape it shows Lil Mack , TJ, Steele , Lil Red and Trae Trae entering the hospital and it also show the license plates on the car and the driver speeding out at a high rate of speed detective Williams rewinded the tape to get a better look at the driver Chris kept looking at the face but couldn't remember where the face was from he told detective Williams to go run a check on the license while he looked at the tape some more he kept rewinding but was interrupted by detective Williams telling him that the plates came back to the car was to a person Sam sims aka Steele his address 3401 west florist street he is a convicted felony been to prison 3 times on all drugs and murder charges Chris reply was I knew the mother fucker I sent his ass to prison all times he from the north side he worked for the biggest gang in the city the bloods now let's suit up and go by his house hopefully we can locate the car call all units and tell them to meet us there in case this get ugly . Steele was at home chilling he was on the phone with trae trae he was feeling good because Trae Trae was telling him that they would be released from the hospital soon he also told him that one of the detective just left the room saying Lil Mack didn't make it he died having surgery this shit crazy Steele told him everything would be ok just be strong Steele told him if it was the last thing he do in life Icy and Tim going to die trae trae cut Steele off saying you just don't understand what will I tell Lil Mack momma she been calling back to back now he dead and I got to delivery the bad news then they want let nobody come see me you know them crackers don't like me I know they going to take me in I haven't heard from lil red and TJ I hope they still downstairs Steele cut him off saying just relax bro that shit happened all too fast I'm glad you ok I'm about to call a meeting with the bloods call when you released I just hope your lil cousin Lil Red don't say shot I know TJ solid but you know how woman get down before Steele could say anything else he heard his front door being kicked in all Trae Trae heard on the phone was police get down or we will shoot and the phone hung up trae trae hit the hospital bed saying fuck all he could think about is how shit went from good to bad fast. Steele was on the ground with his hands on his head detective Chris walked over and cuff Steele he told him yea you thought you got away Steele gave Chris a funny look and silence the whole way to the car. Chris read him his rights. As of now, you're being arrested for tampering with the evidence. We not going to search your house. The warrant is only for you and that car that's covered up in your backyard. So why did you leave the hospital? Steele's reply was because I was scared! You see all my people shot at the hospital I'm plus I don't talk to the police. I need my lawyer! Any other questions?! Detective Chris replied ok but you going to the station and walked off. Detective Williams and Detective Oliver called the tow truck to come get the car while waiting they were taking pics of all the evidence in the car and searched for any further possible leads but only can't up with bullet holes in the car and two cellular phones.

CHAPTER 25

Icy and Porsha walked into the house to find Levelle still up watching tv soon as Icy saw Levelle he gave him a hug he was glad that he didn't die because he had an obligation to upload with his sister that passed away. Levelle asked Icy what was wrong and where Tim was. Icy reply was he was at the hospital. We got shot that's why I'm limping. He could see the rage in Levelle eyes. He looked up at his Uncle Icy with tears in his eyes and his exact words were, "I'm going to kill them pussy ass niggas! Who did this to you Unc?!" Icy told him don't worry about it and that it's already handled and that they just got to make sure Tim is good. Levelle looked at Icy and asked him where uncle Tim get shot at. Icy reply was, in the stomach and some other spots he wasn't sure about. Porsha began calling Icy name telling him his bath water was ready. Icy told Levelle to relax he was going to show up and come holler back at him. They gave each other dap and icy limped to the bathroom. When he made it, Porsha helped him take his clothes off and sat him in the warm water. She kissed him and told him she loved him to death. His reply was, I love you too baby and you've always been by my side even when shit got bad. You were always there. Her reply was, bae I'm going to always ride with my man no matter what. We locked in. Levelle was in the front calling his main man Carlos but he still wasn't answering. Levelle tried calling once more but it was still no answer. He realized it was 5:00 am so he assumed Carlos was still asleep. Icy took a shower and went laid down. Porsha rolled a blunt and cut the tv on. She asked Icy was he hungry. His reply was, yes bae. You're about to cook? Her reply was, yes I will be back. Porsha went and prepared a full meal within 40 mins. She cooked pancakes, sausages, eggs, and rice. When she was done fixing the plates she told Levelle his plate was on the table and headed to the room where Icy was. He was sitting in the chair watching First 48. Porsha walked up to him and gave him his plate and a kiss. She told him to never scare her again and she love him for life. His reply was bae I love you too but I still need you to do me that favor. I just need this one lick and I'm done. I promise! I got like $100,000 put up and I will spend that I'm no time. I just need something to fall back on. I got to get Levelle a car and make sure he good, plus a new house. We already got too much going on. I know them pussy ass niggas gone try to come back and catch us slipping so we have to be ready. Porsha's reply was ok. She didn't want to tell him that she went off on Biggs and fucked the lick up. She was going through too much to have Icy mad at her.

CHAPTER 26

Vasha was at the hospital still sitting beside Tim's side. He had woken up and was able to talk a little bit. His speech was still not clear due to the tubes that ran down his throat. Vasha leaned over kissed him and told him to relax and that she love him to death. When he heard her speak tears rolled down his eyes. She saw the tears and wipe his face. She told him don't cry you are going to be ok. They both were crying. They were interrupted by the nurses coming in. When the nurse came in she told Vasha her name was Nurse Green and she was there to take care of Tim and make sure he have a successful recovery. She also told Vasha that the surgery went well and the tubes will be removed tomorrow morning. Vasha jumped up and gave the nurse a big hug and told her thank you so much with tears in her eyes. The nurse couldn't do anything but cry as well. Detective Chris was calling Vasha's phone none stop so she stepped into the hallways to take the call. When she answered he filled her in on everything and every possible lead that he could find. He told her that Steele was at the police station and the car that pulled off from the hospital had been recovered.

He also told her it was filled with bullet holes. Vasha's reply was has anyone talked yet? Chris's reply was I haven't interviewed them yet but the other detective have and couldn't get a word out of them and you know Steele lives by the street code so at this time we have nothing but a shot-up car and two cell phones. Vasha's reply was cut them all loose. We have nothing to hold them on but keep the car for evidence. I will call you later she said. Chris replied, "ok" and they ended the call. When Detective Chris got off the phone he told detective Williams and Oliver to release them all under pending investigation, but he need to head to the hospital to interview Terrance aka Trae Trae. He also said, "we really can't charge anyone until we get some more leads. I know they will fuck up soon and we will have their ass." The detectives did what they were told. They walked into the next room and removed the handcuffs. Trae Trae was sitting on the hospital bed when he heard Detective Chris walk into the room. He was the last person he wanted to see but he knew he had to face the fact at some point. Chris walked in and got straight to the point. I don't have time to BS around today. You know why I'm here so tell me. I need to know who the fuck shot you and killed your friend? Trae Trae's reply was, I don't know. Somebody did a drive-by but missed me. When I know you, will know. Chris's reply was, you young punks keep living by the street code it's going to be plenty more people dead. Sooner or later we will catch y'all and when we do y'all ass is grass. 6 people just got killed we know Lil Red is your cousin. Shame on the bastard who killed them. We can't prove that this is a connection yet but believe me, we watching. Here go my card. Call me ASAP when you heard something. Trae Trae's reply was, I will never call you! I don't talk to pigs! Chris kept walking like he didn't hear a word he said. Chris walked into Tim's room to find Vasha laying back in her chair next to Tim. When she saw Chris she lifted up asking him was everything ok? His reply was, yea I'm about to head home. It's been a long night. Vasha's reply was, ok I'm about to get some rest as well I will call you when I get up. Chris's reply was ok. What are the doctors saying? Vasha replied he will be ok. They taking the tubes out tomorrow and they say the surgery when well. Chris replied that's good call me if you need me and walked out of the room. Trae Trae walked out of the hospital with murder on his mind he called Lil Red's phone and told her he would call her when he woke up. He also told her to put Steele on the phone. Steele got on the phone and told him bro I'm headed to the house. I got TJ with me so he can get some rest. Trae Trae's reply was, yea tell cuz to call his mom. She has been calling none stop. Steele replied he just got off the phone with her. Shit crazy blood! We got to ride on them niggas asap! Trae Trae's reply was you know that! I'm just glad them pigs let us go. They say they got the car? Steele's reply was yeah. I was moving so fast and put it in the back yard but wasn't shit in there. But call me later, I will be at the house. Trae Trae reply ok blood and ended the call.

CHAPTER 27

Icy woke up with his side hurting. Porsha was next to him and she could tell he was in pain. She handed him the hydros that she had in her purse. She popped them from time to time when she was up on her days off and needed some rest. Icy took the pill and tried to get up but he was in too much pain and too weak to move. He called Levelle's name and told him to come here. Levelle walked into the room with the phone in his hand saying what up Unc? Icy reply was shit just checking on you. We are about to go see Tim in the minute so get ready. Levelle reply was ok and walked back into the living room. Icy looked down at his phone and noticed he had 5 missed calls from ox he called him back the phone rang 2 times and ox picked up what's up Lil bro? I have been calling to check on you I knew you were sleeping. Icy reply was hell yeah I woke up hurting like a bitch ox replied hell yeah you going to be sore for a min but you're a rider you going to be good but look I'm about to head over to the hospital where you at I will scoop you up? Icy replied over Porsha's house you know the condos on Sanford? Ox's reply was say less I will be pulling up in 15 mins and they ended the call. Icy got off the phone and told Porsha that Ox was about to come take him and Levelle to the hospital she was looking crazy because she didn't want them to leave he had just gotten shot but she understood he had to look after Tim her reply was ok bae be careful and here go the key so y'all can come straight in. Vasha woke up to the nurses changing Tim's bandages again due to the womb they had to get changed 3 times a day she looked at Tim and could tell he was in pain it jutted her heart to see him like that when she saw him move she knew he was ok she told the nurse that he needed more pain meds the nurse replied I just gave him more meds they should kick in soon Vasha replied okay thank you so much the nurse replied all this my job this is what I get paid for.

CHAPTER 28

Carlos was riding in the car with Lil Fat he was showing Carlos where all the crackheads be in case he wanted to move around a little he even showed him how to bag the crack up the next stop was to show him how to cook it but hey still had 3 sales to make first. Lil Fat pulled up on Trae Trae to cop some work he needed a fresh 9 zips because he had ran out he only had one 8 ball left and the way his phone was rolling it wouldn't last another hour. Trae Trae got in the car with a sling on his arm Fat asked him what happened to him. Trae Trae's reply was nigga you ain't heard about it? That fuck nigga Icy shot me I shot him and Tim ass them niggas robbed me at the club a min ago then niggas killed my cousins but don't worry them niggas gone pay Lil Fat looked at Carlos and shake his head then told Trae Trae you have to be careful out here Trae Trae reply was I got me out here I got me Lil Fat gave Trae Trae $8,000 for the 9 zips and Trae Trae gave him the work. Lil Fat asked him was the work good because the last time it was cut up. Trae Trae's reply was I forgot you called me back here go $500 back but that's the real deal right there and call me soon as you cook it. Lil

Fat replied ok homies stay up. Trae Trae got out of the car and was heading back to the driveway Carlos got out of the car to take a piss he didn't tell Lil Fat because he knew Lil Fat didn't even know he had his 40 Glock on him Carlos ran up behind Trae Trae and shot him 3 times in the head then took the bag of money that held the money and took off running back to the car when he made it to the car Lil Fat jumped and asked what the fuck going on? Carlos's reply was fuck that nigga he talk too much and plus that nigga shot Unk. You know that's my people and any nigga cross my family going to die. Lil Fat was driving so fast he was acting scared but Carlos didn't give a fuck. If he had anything to say Carlos was ready to blast his ass too. Carlos told Lil Fat to drop him off at home and stop driving so fast! Lil Fat's reply was ok bro. I'm just trying to get away. Did you make sure you kill that niggas because we don't need the police looking for us? Carlos's reply was man I shot that nigga in the head 3 times. You just keep your mouth shut or you will get the same business. Lil fat replied bro I'm with you all the way fuck that nigga I didn't even know you were about to do that shit Carlos reply was me neither it just happened Lil Fat said boy your ass crazy before they could talk some more they were pulling up to Carlos house before getting Carlos told Lil Fat to make sure he doesn't say shit to anybody. Lil Fat's reply was you know I'm solid and drove off. Carlos ran straight to his room he was scared and happy at the same time he called Levelle's phone it rang two times and

Levelle answered what it do bro? Carlos replied shit where Icy at? Levelle reply was he in the room we about to go see Tim but what's wrong with you bro I can tell something wrong? Carlos's reply was bro I just killed that nigga Trae Trae I was with Lil fat and we pulled up on his bitch ass he was bragging about shooting Unk them tell Unk to hurry up and come get me? Levelle's reply was, hold on I'm bout to go give him the phone don't be playing.When Levelle made it to the room Icy and Porsha had just finished wrapping his leg up when he looked up he noticed Levelle standing there Icy asked him was he ok? Levelle's reply was I need to holla at you bout something important in private. Icy told Porsha to let him holla at his nephew real quick Porsha walked out and closed the door. Levelle gave the phone to Icy soon as said hello Carlos got straight to it Unk I just killed that nigga Trae Trae come pick me up. Icy replied who is this Carlos? Carlos's reply was yes I will tell you when y'all get here I'm at home icy replied don't go anywhere I'm on my way abs hung up the phone. Icy looked at Levelle and asked him to do you tho he playing? Because I don't have time to fuck around my brother sitting in the hospital fighting for his life and I'm shot the fuck up. Levelle's reply was naw Unk he's for real. He said he was with lol fat and saw Trae Trae and he was running off at the mouth we need to hurry up and get to him before he does something stupid Icy reply was let me call that nigga Ox and see where he at. Icy called Ox's phone it rang two times. Ox picked up and said I'm outside I just pulled up. Icy reply was we coming downstairs now and hung up. Icy jumped up got his crutches and hopped to the front room Porsha was coming out of the bathroom. Icy stopped her kissed her and said to her, "go do what I told you to do. I need this shit done ok." Porsha's reply was I got you, baby, let me go by Peaches house. Icy reply was fuck that! Do what the fuck I told you! Fuck Peaches... It's too much going on! Porsha's reply was ok baby I'm bout to do it now. I love you! Icy please calm down okay? His reply was, just do what I told you and we will be back later. He and Levelle walked out the door.

CHAPTER 29

Police cars were everywhere when Detective Chris made it to the crime scene Detective Williams and Oliver was talking to Trae Trae's mom she was screaming, cursing, and fighting try to get around the yellow tape the detectives were trying to calm her down she kept repeating the same words over and over "not my baby Lord! Not Terrance! Please I need my son! Please Lord help me Please!" A car pulled up and stopped on the brakes so hard. The police almost drew their guns until they saw two ladies getting out it was Mrs. Carolin and Lil Red Carolin was Trae Trae's aunt she broke down to see her sister cry she wrapped her arms around her everything going to be ok while walking her to the car the whole scene was sad Lil red started screaming and crying she couldn't believe her cousin was dead Detective Chris walked up to her wrapping his arms around her and said all you have to do is tell us who did the shooting earlier you see this not going to stop calm down talk to me the more Chris talked the louder Lil red cried it hurt her soul to see her favorite cousin gone here it was she grieving over her brother now her cousin. Chris told

Detective Oliver to handle Lil Red he was trying to interview a witness who said they saw Trae Trae get out of the car. Then a younger boy with a hoodie on got out the car and started shooting but his face was Coby so he didn't see his face but the car was a blue Dodge Charger Chris told the witnesses to come sit in the back seat of his car he asked him what his name? The witness replied Brandon Foots Sir. Chris sat him in the back seat of the police car and told him to hold still. The officer cut on the a/c then locked the doors and walked back up to the crime scene. When he made it to the corner and other officers were picking up Trae Trae's body the forensic was picking up shell casings that were laying around Trae Trae's body.

CHAPTER 30

Porsha pulled up at Peaches house and called her phone the phone rang three times and Peaches picked up Porsha said girl we're you? I'm sitting outside your house. Peaches replied girl I'm in here I'm in the house I'm trying to get up that young ass nigga wore me out come to the door girl and ended the call. Porsha walked to the door and it was already open. Porsha walked in Peaches room she was in the shower she could hear the water running so say on the chair went into her purse and pulled out some weed she begin rolling up a blunt by the time she was finishing Peaches was walking out of the bathroom she had a towel around her head and a towel around her body she went sat on her bed to lotion up while putting the lotion on she began her storytelling girl let me tell you about this young nigga fucked me so good and ate my pussy all night Porsha reply was so you mean to tell me you rape that little boy like that? They both laughed Peaches reply was girl he's grown as fuck he kept begging so I rocked his little world but on some for real shit what's going on with Icy and Tim? how are they both doing? Porsha's reply was Icy told me, Tim, doing better but Icy is still on the same shit he is on his way to the hospital to check on Tim's ass Peaches looked at Porsha strange well you know Trae Trae just got killed you ain't heard? Porsha reply as hell naw I ain't heard but I know for sure Icy didn't do that shit he been at home but in her head, she was thinking about when Levelle rushed in the room and told Icy he needed to talk to him she knew something wasn't right how Icy ass jumped straight up. Peaches broke her out of the trance that she was in so are you coming to work tonight bitch? Porsha's reply was yeah I missed last night so I got to get this money tonight girl she fired up the blunt took three pulls and passed it to peaches.

CHAPTER 31

Vasha was on the phone with detective Chris when Icy, Ox, Levelle, and Carlos walked through the door of the hospital Tim was sitting up eating the food the nurse had made a feeding tube which was the only way Tim could eat. Vasha stepped outside when she saw all of them walk in to talk to Chris he was telling her about the murder with Terrence aka Trae Trae Vasha's reply was what leads do we have? Chris's reply was I have a witness down here by the name of Brandon Foots he say he saw a younger boy get out a blue charger and fire three shots I released him after I showed him a lineup of Icy and his nephew Levelle he said he couldn't see because the person had a hoodie on I also put an alert out on every blue charger on the streets Vasha reply was ok I'm about to head home I will call you when I make it I need to rest up I will be at work tomorrow and we can go over all details and hung up the phone. Vasha walked back into the hospital room where Tim was sitting she couldn't tell he was happy to see all the love he had flooded the room she kiss him on the forehead and told him she would be back tomorrow she needed to get some rest he couldn't talk so he gave her two thumbs up before leaving she told Icy to step in the hallway he followed her to the hallway before she could speak he told her thanks for looking out for my brother and what did the doctor say about his condition? Vasha's reply was they taking the tubes out his throat tomorrow so he should be good I'm just glad he didn't end up with a colostomy bag and he's still alive but I called you out here to tell you Trae Trae is deceased they say somebody in a blue dodge charger killed him the witness said it was a young boy but the witness see his face y'all be careful please now I'm going home to get some rest Icy reply was thanks, sis, we will see you tomorrow she replied with a strange look and walked off singing love songs.

CHAPTER 32

Biggs and Dollar were at Biggs's house chilling when he saw his phone ring Porsha's name flash across the screen he let the phone ring about three times then picked it up he started not to answer but he couldn't do her like that Biggs picked up talking sweet what up baby? Porsha's reply was nothing do you miss me yet? And we're you at Biggs reply was nothing at the house her reply was I'm about to come by there and you better not gave my dick up?Biggs reply was stop playing with me you know this dick yours laughing and ended the call.When Biggs ended the call he looked at Dollar that was Porsha's crazy ass I knew she was going to call sooner or later I told you I ain't chasing no female "I'm the catch "Dollar started laughing your ass crazy sound just like a groupie Biggs reply was naw I'm for real I took your advice I ain't chasing shit Trina been had her ass over here two nights I been killing her ass really Lil mama cool as fuck she ain't been on that bugging ass shit lately either shit gone be my way or they gone move the fuck around Dollar start's laughing again Nigga you ain't Nemo brown but look I'm about to go. I got to get back to the grind. You know shit don't stop with me. Biggs's reply was ok call me in the morning bro. Dollar's reply was ok bro and walked out of the house. When Dolla left Biggs took a couple of shots of Hennessy cleaned the house rolled a couple of blunts he cut the stereo on Bluetooth to his phone and put it on Lil baby he loved the song no friends he rolled up two blunts fired one up he heard a knock at the door he looked at his phone saw a text from Porsha stating she was outside.Biggs opened the door for her she walked in looking sexy as hell she walked into the house shut the door and start kissing Biggs when she took her Gucci coat off she had nothing on under it and some red button shoes on she walked in the house shut the door and started kissing on Biggs when she took the coat off she had nothing but lingerie on he couldn't do anything but get a hard on Porsha asked him did he miss her? His reply was hell yeah baby but you know that. He fired up a blunt and poured a shot of Hennessy. The song Red Light comes on by Def Loaf and Jacques comes banging through the speakers he couldn't resist her. She was looking and touching him very seductively. Porsha took her shot of Hennessy and lead Biggs to the back room. She lit the backwoods up took a couple pulls then proceeded to take off her clothes. She pulled down his pants and started sucking his dick and playing with his balls for about 10 minutes. He could take it any longer. He took his clothes off and told Porsha to jump on top. She did what she was told she slid his pole deep in while standing on her tiptoes riding him fast and then slow. Biggs was sucking on her neck and slapping her on the ass. Porsha was moaning and screaming his name. She even turned around and started riding him backward and twerking at the same time. Porsha felt herself about to cum so she sped up. Biggs felt a Nut about to come. so he made her get up. He bend her over and was hitting her ruff then slow from the back. Porsha was climaxing everywhere! She was moaning and biting her bottom lip. Biggs was still hitting her from the back until he nutted and he could tell he was cum'n because she went faster and clapped her ass. She came on him as well. Cum was everywhere. When they got done Biggs crashed on the bed looking up at Porsha. She laid on top of him and asked him did he miss her. Hell yeah, baby she replied I missed you too baby I was just mad. I couldn't wait to get back to my dick I'm falling in love with you Biggs I just don't want to get hurt. Biggs looked at Porsha baby I'm not trying to hurt you I'm falling for you as well you just got to trust me and trust the process you know I Love everything I loved I'm trying to build something with you baby. Porsha replies okay baby I've been doing a-lot of thinking about you lately.I just want somebody good I told my brother about you he gets out next year. He said he heard about you want Me to fuck you with the chick from the restaurant I will I want to show you that I'm down for you baby Biggs replied .okay baby but are we still going out of town? Porsha replies year but I have to work tonight so can leave this Friday. I will let my boss know what's up but where are we going baby? Biggs replied Vegas Baby you ain't gotta worry about packing. I'm taking you shopping when we get there. Porsha replied, okay I can't wait l. She got up and told Biggs she had to get home to take a shower for work Biggs replied baby but come back when you get off. Porsha replica okay she put her clothes on kissed him and walked to the door. When she got in her car she called Icy. the phone rang twice and he picked up saying what's up baby? Porsha replied Nothing just left that Nigga house. Everything is good, he taking me to Vegas on Friday so be ready. I been had his alarm code and I will know where the work at so y'all can go straight in. I will tell you everything, tomorrow baby. I will call you when I get off work Icy please be careful out there. These streets don't love Nobody and Make sure Levelle goes to school.He hasn't been to school in 3 days now love you bye and they ended the call.

CHAPTER 33

(The Next day)

Vasha woke up to her phone steady ringing. It was 10:00 in the morning she didn't have to go in today so she wondered who it was steadily calling. When she looked at the screen she noticed it was the number she saved Icy name under. She answered the phone saying hello. Icy replied well good morning to you too. They just took the tubes out of Tim. They are going to release him at 4:00. You get some rest and I will bring him straight home. Vasha replied "Nah I will be up there at 2:00. I don't need y'all making no extra stops. Plus I need to talk to the nurse to make sure I have everything right about changing his bandages." Icy replied girl shut up and get some rest ain't Nobody thinking about making no extra stops and started laughing Vasha replied ain't Nothing funny you know how y'all Niggas are. I almost snapped when I came in the room and that bitch peaches stripper ass was holding his hand I know she a slut. Icy replica ain't Nobody studying that girl but I will be here when you get here. And he ended the call, Vasha couldn't sleep knowing Tim was getting released from the hospital so she got up fixed her something to eat, and got everything ready for her shower. When she was done eating the burger and fries she looked she Cleaned up the house and put on a load of clothes she wanted everything to be done so all her focus could be on Tim. Vasha finished everything and took her a shower. She tried to take a long shower but her mind kept going back to Tim. She was glad he was okay and she hoped that he was done with the streets. She had known him her whole life and her love ran deep for him so losing him would be too devastating. she know he wouldn't listen if she tried to talk to him but she was doing everything in her power to talk some sense into his head. Vasha got out of the shower put on her clothes said a prayer and headed out the door heading to the hospital. When Vasha made it to the hospital, there were two Nurses in the room. Icy was sitting next to Tim and their nephew levelle and his little friend was sitting in the other chairs. when

Icy saw Vasha enter the room he told the Nurses to explain everything to Vasha so she would know how to clean everything so Tim's healing will go great. The Nurses introduced their self and went on to explain everything to Vasha. When they were done talking, Vasha thanked them and said she appreciate everything that they have done for Tim. The Nurses replied, it's our job. Now let us go turn the paperwork in to the doctors so we could get him released and they walked out of the room. Vasha walked over to Tim and kissed him on the lips. She

PLAY NO GAMES MAKE NO MISTAKES

told him to relax and that she would make sure that he would be okay. Tim Could barely talk because his throat was still sore but he spoke in a light tone and said I love you baby. Icy started laughing and before she could reply Vasha asked Icy what he was laughing at. Icy said y'all two love birds. I can't wait until that Nigga heal up so I can tell him about himself. Know they need to hurry up and release him we've been up here all night and ain't ate nothing. Vasha's reply was y'all can leave, I got him. we will call you when we make it home. Icy reply was okay, I'm about to take these lil Niggas to get them a bite to eat make sure you call me okay? Vasha replied okay before Levelle left out the door, he gave Vasha a hug and Carlos spoke to her and they walked out. when Icy Levelle and Carlos Made it to the car he pulled his phone out and Noticed he had 3 Missed calls from Porsha so he called her phone back. it rang two times and she picked up saying hello baby where are you? Icy reply was just left the hospital they about to release Tim I'm about to get Something to eat and head home you must just woke up? Porsha's reply was yes I'm about to get in the shower bring me something to eat when you come home baby? Icy replied okay and hung up the phone. When icy got off the phone, he told Carlos to call Lil fat phone he gotta holla at him. Carlos's reply was okay and he dialed the number. Lil fat answered the second ring saying what it do lil bro? Carlos said Nothing Much, look, Icy want to holler at you and gave him the phone Icy got the phone and said what it do lil homie? Lil fat replied nothing trying to get this money how about you? Icy replied nothing aye do me a favor. Put your car up. The police looking for it. I will give you $10,000 to get a new car. Meet me in the hood in 1 hour and keep your mouth shut and don't repeat what you saw. You my lil nigga, I know your whole family. I would hate to take it there because I got love for but I ain't with that snitch shit at all. Do you feel me? Lil Fat replied I feel you, but I already put the car in the paint shop. I told Kim to paint it white and I got my people to change

the tags and 06. I have never been a rat! That nigga Trae Trae did what he did now he paid the price so fuck him. I will be in the hood in an hour so we can talk face-to-face. Icy replied okay meet me at the pack and hung up. Icy pulled up to Wing Stop he told Levelle and Carlos to come in so they could get something to eat. They got out of the car and walked in. when they made it to the counter he told the clerk to give him the family box all mixed

Wings Combo the clerk told him it will be so dollars and it will be a 25 min wait. Icy paid the clerk and told Levelle and Carlos to come on and they walked to the car. when they got in the car Jay fired up a blunt of 06 gas. he took a couple of pulls and told Carlos that was some real shit that you did. Me and Tim will never forget that. Now don't go around bragging, and if you have dreams that's normal. Now here go $1,000 lil nigga, go shopping. He talked to him for about 20 mins filling them in on the ins and outs of life. they were soaking up every word. Levelle got out of the car, got the food, and got back in the car. The whole way home Icy kept talking to them until they pulled up at Porsha's house. When they made it to Porsha's house she was cleaning up, washing dishes, and listening to slow music. When she saw Jay she gave him a hug and a kiss and told him she loves him. She grabbed the bags of food out of his hand and sat them on the table. She told Levelle and Carlos to sit down and that she would fix their plates. Icy walked to the room and called Vasha's phone. He needed to check on Tim to make sure he was good. the phone rang twice and Vasha picked up. Hey Icy I was just about to call you we made it home/I'm about to wash him up so if you want to come over we at the house. Icy replied okay sis I will be over later I'm about to take a nap for a minute. tell that crybaby I said I love love him laughing and ended the call. when Icy hung up the phone Porsha was walking into the room with them she handed Icy his plate and sat down on the bed Next to him and started eating. he was eating the food like he haven't eaten in days Porsha looked at him and told him to slow down. Icy reply was shut up hell I'm starving and started laughing. she was laughing too. they kept eating until the food was gone. when Ivy was finished, Porsha grabbed his plate and took it into the kitchen. When she got back he was firing up a blunt. Soon as she sat down, he asked her so what's up with that nigga Biggs and why are you just now telling me you got his house code? Porsha's reply was because I was trying to make sure I had everything lined up baby. so he taking me to Vegas Friday I'm sure he's going to leave the work and Money laying around. This nigga thinks he's untouchable. He will never know it was me he would think it was one of his homeboys. Last week I went over there & it was some Mexican Nigga over there. They had plenty of money laid on the table and plenty blocks of work so I'm sure he hasn't sold out yet. Icy cut her off, so you saying there was plenty of money and work? Porsha replied yeah baby I wouldn't lie to you nor send you on a blank trip. Icy replied I know, I was just trying to make sure. Biggs was at home talking to Dollar about the trip he and Porsha were about to take. He told him everything would be good with the work. If he run out Biggs gave Dollar house code, 909001. he wrote it down on a piece of paper and told him to screenshot it to his phone. Dollar got up screenshot the paper and saved it in his phone. When they were done he gave Biggs the money he owed him and got more bricks out of the bag on the table. Biggs told him we're down to 10 bricks I'm going to re-up before I leave or I'm going to have Rico meet you at the house. It depends on how fast these two leave. You know they have been blowing my phone up lately. I ain't gone lie Rico been coming threw lately with the best shit around. That nigga should be rich as hell. If he giving us the bricks for 20,000 what do you think he getting them for? Dollar's reply was it ain't no telling big bro but that nigga should be rich. Look while you gone relax your mind. Don't let that girl get too wild on you. What time is y'all leaving tomorrow? Biggs replied, around noon. The flight leaves at 1:00 but I will call you and let you know everything. Dollar replied, okay I'm about to go run through this Shit I will hit later and left heading toward the door. When Dollar left Biggs grabbed the bags of money from all the bricks he sold and started counting it. He knew once he was done he would have $900,000 in total but he had 10 bricks left and Dollar still owed for 5 That was 750,000 still out there. Halfway through counting the money his phone started to ring. He looked at the screen and notices Porsha was calling him. He picked up saying what's up baby ?? Porsha's reply was nothing I'm out doing a little shopping and getting ready for our trip what time to our flight leave tomorrow? Biggs's reply was 1:00 but we need to get there at noon. I told you not to buy anything and that we were going shopping once we land. Porsha's reply was I'm not shopping like that, I'm just buying a couple of girl items, that's it, baby. I will be over later I guess. I will just stay all night with you so we can jump straight up and leave. Biggs reply was okay I will be at the house I'm trying to count up the rest of this money just text Me before you come Porsha replied okay then hung up the phone. Porsha hung up the phone leaned over and kissed Icy. She had the phone on speaker so he could hear the whole conversation to let him know that she wasn't leaving. She got up closed the door and asked him now do you believe me? Icy reply was yes baby I believe you he started kissing her neck and playing with her pussy since she had on a house gown with no panties. Porsha let out a soft moan and told him to hold up. She got up walked to the stereo and cut the music on so Levelle and Carlos wouldn't hear them. When R Kelly boomed through the speakers "Seems Like You Ready" came on. Porsha took off her gown and climbed on top of Icy. He pulled down his pants and put his dick in her. She was riding him fast then slow. They were kissing and he was sucking her titties. They had sex for the next 30 Minutes with R Kelly on repeat. Levelle and Carlos were in the front room chopping it up about how he killed Trae Trae. Levelle asked him do we need to kill Lil fat? Carlos Said nah bro it ain't like that. We've been knowing him too long. Remember he was the one who took us to the guns. He still going to show us the game on the dope side. In the middle of them talking Carlos's phone started ringing. it was Lil Fat so Carlos picked up saying what it do bro? Lil Fat replied nothing at the park waiting on y'all. I have been here for 30 mins waiting. Carlos's reply was Unk ass in there with his girl. We going to call you later on. Ain't No telling how long we going to be here. Lil fat said bet just hit me up and hung up the phone. When Carlos ended the call he told Levelle I told you he was cool that Nigga been at the park waiting on us. If he was on some bullshit he wouldn't be calling us. I got to get another gun you know Unc that one so won't get caught. Your gun is put up at my house. I made sure

I hid it so Mama ass won't find it. So we good. Levelle's reply was hell yeah I'm glad uncle Tim made it through. That would have hurt my soul if he didn't make it out and I'm glad you laid TraTrae down. You see Niggas talk too much. One thing we can't do is run around bragging about people we killed. What's understood ain't got to be explained.

THE END

Made in the USA
Columbia, SC
28 January 2023